The Alphabet Man

Barrie McCappin

The Alphabet Man
ISBN: 978-1-4717-3971-2
First publication in www.lulu.com
Copyright © Barrie McCappin 2012

Barrie McCappin has asserted his right under the Copyright, Designs and Patents Act 1988 to be identified as the author of this work.

In this work of fiction, the characters, places and events are either the product of the author's imagination or they are used entirely fictitiously. Any resemblance to actual persons living or dead, is purely coincidental.

Although the persons shown on the cover depict the characters in the book, they are used purely for illustration, the author having gained their unequivocal consent to be photographed and used on the cover. These persons do not in any way represent the nature or portray the lifestyle of those depicted within the content of the book.

This book is sold subject to the condition that it should, by way of trade or otherwise, be leant, resold, hired out, or otherwise circulated without the publisher's prior consent in any form of binding or cover other than that in which it is published and without a similar condition including this condition being imposed on the subsequent purchaser.

Barrie J McCappin was born in December 1940 at Aveley, Essex and now lives with his wife Daisy at Canvey Island. In the course of his working life he took occupations with firms of professional Quantity Surveyors and Building Contractors where he was employed on a number of large building and civil engineering projects. Now in retirement the Author spends his time in using his previous occupational skills in 'do it yourself' property enhancement and travelling. Author of the books 'Time for Change' and 'Blue Diamond', he continues to write novels on fictitious situations in epochs within the twentieth and twenty first centuries.

Previous Works   Time for Change   2011

                     Blue Diamond   2012

This Book is dedicated to Jeffrey Salisbury

                         Clare Salisbury

                         Gemma O'Malley

Chapter 1 Spencer

To Spencer Henry Andrews, the world was a magical place of women and lust. Wherever he went he would constantly look around and his eyes would be magnetised to any beautiful woman irrespective of age that appeared in his visual vicinity. As a sexual predator he would then target and stalk his prey in an attempt to gain attention from the person who attracted his interest.

Spencer rarely had a problem in achieving any goal he set himself where women were concerned. He was blessed with a tremendous advantage in being epitomised as a perfect example of the male species. As a result, the man did not need to try too hard in order to attract the opposite sex. At age twenty five, this bachelor was a strapping six feet three inches in height weighed approximately two hundred pounds, had broad shoulders, a slim waist, brown hair, French cropped close to the head and hazel eyes. Being a lorry driver, his work took him to all parts of the country and abroad, which for Spencer proved to be a great advantage, because he was never in any place long enough to develop a serious attachment with any woman who wanted more than a brief courtship. Spencer certainly wasn't one for settling down with a permanent partner, at least he thought he wasn't. To do this would interrupt his serial conquests and brief liaisons which had become his general pattern of life.

Little did Spencer know it, but his single ways were to come to a dramatic end and his future destined to be engulfed in family life. If Spencer could have read the future, he would have undoubtedly have approached life differently, taking care not to involve himself with so many women.

Spencer's only family was his mother and father who lived in Devonshire. His parents tried desperately to try to control him. In order to escape their strict guidance, he moved out of the family house at the young age of nineteen years and put a deposit on a small bungalow just outside Birmingham. He treated women with disdain, saw them not as people, but of objects of delight. However he did display some attributes which complimented his character. Whatever he embarked on he would carry out to the best of his ability and he would never knowingly let anyone down.

Spencer's life changed on one very hot day in June. He had just unloaded his lorry in Birmingham and decided to call in a local cafe for a tea and light refreshment. The cafe being a grubby place was half full, the main clientele being motorists. Spencer quickly found himself a seat in the middle of the eating house. In the process of sipping his tea, in walked a truly beautiful woman aged approximately twenty three years with a stunning figure. Her height was five feet three inches; she had blond mid length straight hair and deep blue eyes. She ordered a coffee and sat at the adjacent table. Spencer couldn't take his eyes off her, gazing at her like some lovesick teenager as he munched noisily into his cupcake.

Spencer's attempts to converse with the girl, who quickly realised that she was about to be propositioned looked away to demonstrate her disinterest. Spencer, who with his vast experience with women, had witnessed these behavioural patterns in the past, was not phased by the girls manner, but instead saw it as a challenge which needed careful management and had to be pursued. Without any further hesitation, he left his seat and sat uninvited opposite the girl on her table.

'My name's Spencer but I don't know your name,' he said as he tried to attract her interest.

The girl gave no answer and continued to show her disinterest and didn't even look in Spencer's direction but gazed around at the empty walls.

'Look,' said Spencer, 'we can't sit at the same table and ignore each other. People in here will start looking at us and making us the subject of their conversations.'

The girl who was still looking away suddenly altered her gaze to confront Spencer.

'I never asked you to join me on this table and therefore I have nothing to say to you, so you can crawl back to the table that you have just left. I have no wish to talk to you,' said the girl.

'Well that's a start. At least I've got you talking to me,' said Spencer with a smile, who was not at all concerned that it wasn't the answer he was looking for.

The girl remained silent. Spencer looked around the cafe and noticed that since he moved to her table, almost all the seats had been taken, even those on the table he left. He saw this as an advantage, because he couldn't return to the recently occupied table that he had left. All he had to do was to put in process a bit of clever play acting.

'The cafe is filling up now and if I was to move to another table, you could get someone sitting opposite you who would annoy you more than me,' said Spencer who was in no position to give up his quest for dating this girl.

At that moment, a woman entered the cafe with two young boys about the ages of eight and nine. Both these kids were carrying toy water pistols and yelling abuse at the mother. Spencer immediately saw his opportunity and stood up to vacate his seat.

'These seats are available,' he said to the obnoxious family with the behavioural problems that had just walked in.

'No!' said the girl to Spencer, after having glanced at the new arrivals entering the cafe, 'don't go, please sit down,' she begged Spencer.

'Oh, so you can put up with me after all,' said Spencer.

Spencer's play acting seemed to work and he gladly followed the girls request and retained his seat and composure.

'My name is Glenda and I'm pleased to meet you Spencer,' said the girl as she raised her arm for a handshake.

Spencer now knew that he had broken the ice with this girl called Glenda and was then able to proceed with the standard banter he had adopted and used on all his other female achievements. However he sensed that with Glenda, who was a bit more worldly wise, this was going to be a bit more difficult to manipulate than his previous conquests. Nevertheless, Spencer thrived on a challenge as it made the ultimate success far more worthwhile.

He began by asking her, what interests she had in life, what she did for a living, whether she had a boyfriend or not, did she live locally and finally having established a satisfactory approval of her answers, a request for her telephone number.

The silver tongue used by Spencer seemed to work its magic and it wasn't long before Spencer had won Glenda over and arranged to make a date with her. The first date was a huge success. Spencer was captivated by this girl and continued dating her on a regular basis.

However Spencer being Spencer did not stop with one woman, he had to indulge himself with a whole harem of women spread across the country. He would see Glenda on one day and another woman on the following day, and continue alternating his female liaisons with the aid of a well kept diary. At all times doing his best to keep his cheating exploits secret.

Five months after he first met Glenda, Spencer happened to be in the Birmingham area and called in to see her. He hadn't seen Glenda in a while, but the greeting he received was not exactly a warm welcome.

'You fool,' said Glenda who dispensed with the usual introductory pleasantries, 'you've made me pregnant.'

Glenda was in tears and banging her fists on Spencer's chest. Spencer having suffered enough pounding to the chest gently eased Glenda away from him.

'Are you sure?' asked Spencer, 'there could be some mistake.'

'There's no mistake,' said Glenda still in tears, 'I've just had a scan done in the hospital and they are twins.'

Spencer was mortified at hearing this revelation, especially the bit about twins and was totally lost for words.   He had never been faced with a situation like this in the past and therefore was not sure how to handle it.

'So what are you going to do about it?' asked Glenda.

'There is not much I can do,' said Spencer who was stunned by the full realisation of the situation.

'I thought you would say that.   I suppose now that you know, you will run away and I will never see you again,' said Glenda still in tears.

'What sort of a person do you think I am?' said Spencer pretending to be hurt by her suggestion.

'Well then, are you going to stick by me?   Are you still going to continue to see me?' pressed Glenda.

'Of course I will, we will get married,' said Spencer, 'Yes, that's what we will do. We will get married.'

'Are you sure?' asked Glenda. The tears by this time had stopped and replaced with a smile of elation at hearing Spencer's suggestion.

'Yes, I am positive,' replied Spencer, 'but I'm afraid I will have to leave all the wedding arrangements up to you to organise, because of my haphazard work schedule. I'm always on the road and I don't know where I will be from one week to the next.'

Spencer realised that in committing himself to wedlock he had to say goodbye to his bachelor days and concentrate on family life. The knowledge that twins were on the way, now, that was another matter to which he would need complete adjustment to his already hectic life. Did Spencer intend to change his wild ways into something more sedate befitting family life? Only Spencer knew the answer to this question.

Anyone who knew Spencer would have got the distinct impression that he was being pushed towards nuptials which did not receive his complete acceptance. He did nothing towards the preparation of the wedding ceremony leaving the arrangements, such as booking the church and the reception entirely in Glenda's hands. His fiancé tried to involve him, but was always informed that he was far too busy to get entangled with the trivia of processing the arrangements for the big day or the honeymoon.

On the day of the wedding, which was also attended by many of Spencer's lorry driver friends, he was thirty minutes late. This promoted speculation amongst those who knew him well, that he would renege on the ceremony and not turn up at all. However when he finally arrived at the church, the unexpected attendance brought a cheer from the doubted guests.

'Spencer, we thought you weren't going to go through with it,' said one of his workmates.

'Don't think that I didn't give it some thought. That's why I am late,' replied Spencer.

As the ceremony continued, a more disinterested groom could not be imagined. Spencer never raised a smile once. He recited the words verbatim given to him by the priest, without showing any sign of interest or change of intonation of his voice. However to his credit, he did go through with the ceremony, making promises of everlasting fidelity to his spouse which he knew he could never keep.

At the reception, Spencer still retained his expression of displeasure. Glenda on the other hand appeared extremely happy and did not seem to notice Spencer's moodiness. She danced the night away in the company of her guests, rather than use her new husband as a partner. Spencer meanwhile, who did not appear to enjoy the festivities was looking for a way to escape the loud music and drunken antics of the invitees in favour of a quieter option away from the revelling family and guests.

Spencer's lorry driver workers made the most of the occasion by constantly reminding Spencer that his bachelor days were over and goaded him at every opportunity on the respectability of marriage.

Towards the end of the evening, Spencer made his move by announcing that he had to leave the reception because he had to work that evening and wouldn't be back in Birmingham for another three days. Spencer showed no embarrassment when he left his new bride to look after their guests. Instead he heaved a sigh of relief when he left the reception and headed straight for his lorry.

The announcement he made to his surprised bride and guests was a genuine fact. Spencer's friends knew that his boss would have understood the extenuating circumstances for not working on his wedding day, but Spencer had purposely made no attempts to get his work schedule changed.

After the wedding, Spencer managed to settle down in family life and managed to attain some satisfaction from it. Although his work took him to remote parts of the country and abroad, he managed to get home most evenings to enjoy a home life with his wife.

Life was uncomplicated without stress and having said goodbye to his bachelor days he managed to settle down to a regular pattern which balanced work with home life. Spencer even began to enjoy this new way of life which included socialising with a few friends he had made in the neighbourhood.

Spencer managed to keep to the style of his new normality for approximately six weeks, after which time he fell into his old habits of drifting and flirting with other women.

Chapter 2 Holly and Iris

Three months after the wedding, Spencer was in Portsmouth where he met a pretty girl aged approximately twenty two by the name of Holly. She was five feet four inches, dark haired with green eyes. Spencer, although now married, could still charm his prey with the same old standard chat up lines that had served him in good stead in the past.

Spencer in his usual way charmed his way to her bedroom and in so doing placing all the pledges he made to Glenda at his wedding day far from his mind as he romped in Holly's bed. Holly had no idea that Spencer was married which was a secret he wished to keep firmly to himself.

Four months elapsed and the twins were borne to Glenda. Spencer gave Glenda the responsibility for naming the children which was a task he would never involved himself in. The twins were a healthy boy and a girl. Glenda named the boy Malcolm and the girl Norma. Spencer surprisingly made a wonderful father, being very attentive towards the children whenever he saw them, which due to his newly developed busy lifestyle, was not very often.

Unbeknown to Glenda, Spencer was being shared between Holly and her and was the main reason that he was missing most of the time. Spencer was always claiming that his work took him away from the family. Glenda never suspected anything and even began to feel sorry for him, believing that he was missing out on the children growing up.

Five months had elapsed and history was beginning to repeat itself, because Holly was claiming that she was expecting a child in the winter and named Spencer as the father. However, to Spencer's misfortune Glenda was also pregnant expecting for the second time, twins in the following January.

Spencer's mind was in turmoil. He didn't know what to do. He had to talk to Holly and reveal that he was already married with a family of two children and therefore could never see her again. Spencer made a special visit by driving down to Portsmouth and on the way practising the best way of broaching the subject to Holly. When he arrived Holly's father happened to be in the house displaying a distinct mood of discontent.

'This is a fine kettle of fish you've placed my daughter in,' he said angrily.

Holly's father being there, seemed to place a completely different perspective on the situation, because Spencer found himself unable to come out with the revelation that he already had a family. Fearful of what Holly's father might say or do to him, Spencer started to agree with everything he said.

'Well yes,' Spencer said sheepishly, 'I can understand why you are annoyed.'

'Annoyed is putting it mildly,' said Holly's father, 'I of course, expect you to do the honourable thing and marry my daughter, because if you possessed any form of respectability, then that's the only thing you can do in order to give a child a father and stable family life.'

Spencer was about to say that he was already married, but looking at the anger in Holly's father's eyes, thought better about it. Besides Holly's father, whose occupation was the Manager of a bank, had a very persuasive way of putting his points across. Like running a bank, he liked to do everything according to his own book of regulations.

'If you don't do the right thing by my daughter, I will come and seek you out and you my friend will regret the day you were born,' said Holly's father.

Holly's father was a big man with plenty of weight behind him and did not appear to be the type that would make an idle threat.

'Okay, Okay,' repeated Spencer who by then was not only being pushed into nuptials but threatened if he didn't comply. 'There was never any doubt in my mind other than to marry Holly,' said Spencer who looked directly at Holly's father.

Holly's father in hearing the proposal made by Spencer, appeared to be in a more relaxed mood. Spencer then turned to Holly.

'Holly, can I leave it to you to make the wedding arrangements, my work takes me all over the place and I fear I will not be around to give my assistance?'

'Yes, I'll set everything up, but I don't know your surname Spencer,' said Holly.

Spencer knew that in marrying again he couldn't use his real name, so he had to think of an alternative quickly.

'It's Butcher, Holy. Spencer Henry Butcher,' he confirmed.

'Now don't forget what I have told you,' said Holly's father who had now calmed down and even managed a smile.

'No! It's implanted on my mind that if the marriage between your daughter and me does not go ahead you will seek me out. You have no worries Sir I will comply with your wishes,' confirmed Spencer. Holly's father then patted Spencer on the back and his complete attitude changed. He appeared to be uncomfortably over friendly. He started to smile from time to time, even offered Spencer a cigar. It seemed that in offering to marry his daughter, Spencer had turned from a loathsome person to one of his greatest buddies.

Holly's father may not have had any further worries, but Spencer's mind was doing overtime. He was aware that in marrying Holly, he had to break an important law of the land by resorting to bigamy. There was also the extra burden and associated finance attributed to the pending additional children who would shortly be born. Having placated Holly and her father with an offer of marriage, Spencer was glad to leave the Holly household and get back on the road.

The day of the wedding to Holly arrived and true to his word Spencer made sure he was available to go through the process of marital union to satisfy Holly and Holly's father, who had really laid on a ceremony of extreme splendour, where no expense was spared. The bride was supported with six bridesmaids all dressed in pink. Horse drawn carriages brought the bride and bride's family to the church. The reception was equally lavish with a six tier cake and four course meals for all the guests. Holly's mother and father also gave the new bride and groom a three bedroom house to live in after the reception. If Spencer was feeling any guilt at all, he should have felt it then. He certainly felt uncomfortable about receiving all this wealth from Holly's parents, having committed a bogus marriage to their daughter.

After the wedding, Spencer divided his time up between Glenda and Holly, neither of which knew of the other person's existence. Both his partners were aware that his regular absence was taken up by the unsocial hours of his job. This gave him the golden excuse for his regular absence and both wives reasoned that the open road would absorb most of his time. After all what wife could deny him time off for working, even if it did mean staying out over night. By the careful use of alternate dates for visiting his two wives there was no reason why each of his partners would know about the existence of the other one.

Holly's baby was born in December, who was a girl named Olga. Glenda's twins were again a boy and a girl called Quilly and Patricia. Up to this point Spencer had sired five children. Life for Spencer was getting pretty hectic and the money to provide for his two families was becoming increasingly scarce and difficult to manage. The extent of his problems were such that he decided that he would turn over a new leaf in his life, by not embarking on any new love matches, no matter how tempting. As far as Spencer was concerned, women were the catalyst for his problems and from then onwards, female dating would be placed firmly in the past.

Then one day in March, Spencer was required to go to Torbay in Devon. Having unloaded his cargo, he went to one of the local restaurants to eat. He found a table and ordered his meal and while he was waiting for his starter he commenced reading the newspaper. A woman aged approximately twenty seven years entered the establishment.

'Can I sit here with you?' came a female voice.

Spencer looked up and saw an attractive looking woman with dark brown hair and brown eyes approximately five feet five inches in height.

'Help your self,' said Spencer indicating the vacant chair with his hand.

Spencer continued to read his newspaper. The woman sat down and then the waiter turned up with Spencer's starter.

'Yes, that looks nice,' said the woman, 'I think I will order the same.'

Now normally Spencer would be exchanging telephone numbers by this time, but he had kept to the pledge that he had made to himself, not to get involved with anything wearing a skirt, so he remained silent. However, the woman was about to bombard him with questions.

'Do you live around here?' asked the woman.

'No I don't,' Spencer replied as he tucked into a spoonful of prawns. 'Do you?' he replied as he turned the question back to her.

'Yes,' she said, 'I own the Manor that you may have passed on the road if you came from an Easterly direction. I must confess that since my husband died, it has become a bit too large for me to live in on my own.'

Suddenly Spencer became interested and became more attentive towards her. This clearly was a woman of wealth and because of her fortunate status of riches, he had to make an exception to the promise he made to himself. He started to think that the person sitting opposite him at his table could be the answer to all his prayers. Yes, he had to make a concerted effort to get to know her properly. He remembered passing the Manor and although he did not take too much notice of it at the time, he could recall it as a large building with a lot of land around it.

Spencer then turned on his charm and went though all the usual questions, paying particular attention on the answers which indicated wealth. Having made up his mind this woman, who called herself Iris, ticked all his boxes and a lot more besides, decided that she would be an ideal candidate for meeting on a regular basis.

Meeting up on a regular basis was exactly what happened and Spencer wined and dined Iris as often as his circumstances would allow, until Iris had accepted that Spencer was an important part of her life and someone she didn't want to lose. The days turned into weeks and the weeks turned into months and Iris realised that she could not continue a life without Spencer and longed for the day when he would ask her to marry him.

Spencer realised that in order to gain any part of Iris's wealth he had to make the partnership with her more permanent. After all he had committed bigamy once, so it wouldn't cause too much trouble to commit bigamy a second time. Spencer made an unusual step of proposing to a woman, which is something he has never done before. With this woman, the circumstances were different because he wasn't being goaded into marriage like his other two experiences. He was delighted when Iris accepted and as was his usual custom, requested that she make the arrangements for the wedding.

This wedding seemed different to Spencer and the delight on his face indicated his true feelings that he had indeed made a wise choice in picking Iris as his bride.

For the first time Spencer became very nervous when he went to the registry office.

When the Registrar raised the question, 'Does any person here present know any just cause or impediment why these two should not be joined in holy matrimony, let him now speak or forever hold his peace,' Spencer nervously looked round as if someone was going to jump out of nowhere and stop the proceedings. He did however utter a sigh of relief when the Registrar pronounced them man and wife. This pronouncement not only made Spencer a married man for the third time but also gave him fifty per cent share in a Manor. There was also Iris's personal wealth. For although he wasn't aware of the extent of the fortune that she held he had a suspicion that Iris was a woman of considerable means.

After the wedding initially Spencer gave Iris as much time as he could, but as time went by, cosy days at the Manor became more and more remote, as he tried to juggle his time between three wives, neither wishing to offend or afford favour to any one of them.

Chapter 3 Dangerous Weather

Spencer had some washing machines and spin driers that required delivery from Felixstowe in Suffolk to go to Oxford. The weather conditions on the road were mixed with torrential rain and high winds making visibility poor. His high sided vehicle battled against the winds as he drove down the A12 arterial road, first in Suffolk and then its continuation in Essex. He could feel the gusting winds hitting the side of his vehicle and realised that the only way he could stabilise his vehicle against the weather was to drive slowly. He reduced his speed to no more than a crawl, breaking when a heavy gust hit the side of his vehicle.

Passing a heavy vehicle already on its side and a tree that had fallen into the road, Spencer realised that danger was a constant threat. As he continued, wind speeds reached one hundred and ten miles per hour although gusting levels were much higher.

The gusts were the biggest problem because there was no knowing when these were going to strike. These became stronger and more regular with the passing of time, making driving his high sided vehicle, which acted like a sail, extremely precarious. Rather than risk an accident Spencer decided that he would pull into the next lay-by and wait for the storm to calm down. However before he could put his plan into action, a bend in the road coupled with a fierce gust of wind turned his vehicle on its side, throwing Spencer with extreme force against the side door. He heard something break in his body, followed by extreme pain in his arm.

The sound of new domestic white goods in the back of his high sided vehicle could be heard crashing against one another once the equilibrium of his load had changed. This was sufficient in assisting the fall of the vehicle to topple over onto its side. The smell of diesel filled the air and gave concern that the lorry could soon be engulfed in flames. He told himself that he had to get out and clear of the vehicle quickly.

Spencer climbed out of his vehicle as best he could fearful that an explosion could occur at any time, but hampered by the injuries he had sustained when thrown against the side of the vehicle. The extreme pain he was feeling on the left side of his body signalled that he had broken a collar bone and forearm. He called for an Ambulance on his mobile phone which came to his aid within fifteen minutes. Spencer was then carried by stretcher into the Ambulance and paramedics did all they could to make him comfortable. When the Health Vehicle finally left, Spencer looked back at the depressing sight of his lorry which was surrounded with police and wondered if there was anything he could have done differently to avoid his disaster. The Ambulance took him to Accident and Emergency department of Chelmsford hospital where he was given immediate treatment.

After his arm was set in plaster and a sling placed around him to support the broken limb, the pain had subsided slightly, leaving Spencer to think about other important things in his life, namely Glenda, Iris and Holly the three wives he had in his life. Glenda would most certainly have to be informed of her husband's injuries, but was it necessary to inform Holly or Iris. The last thing that Spencer wanted was for all the three wives to come to see him during the scheduled public visiting times. They would surely know about each other if that happened and the whole secret of bigamist marriages would be brought into the open.

However Spencer had a well structured plan. He would arrange that Glenda visit him in the morning and Holly in the afternoon. Both had long journeys to cover before they could see him, so he wasn't sure if either of them would feel that it was worth the travel inconvenience. A decision was made not to tell Iris about the accident, because there was only two visiting times in the day and these had been used up by Glenda and Holly. He thought also that of the three, Iris would have had the longest distance to travel. However, the arrangement which he intended to make with the other two wives would be the perfect solution to stop them meeting each other.

Spencer made his telephone calls to both Glenda and Holly to give them both the visiting times. He then relaxed in his hospital bed aware that he had overcome what potentially could have been a difficult problem.

Eleven o'clock arrived and the visitors piled into the ward, but surprisingly Glenda was not amongst them. Spencer picked up a book to read, believing that he would not get any visitors that day, but he was wrong. Trailing behind the line of people walking through the ward doors was Holly. Spencer got the shock of his life, because Holly wasn't due to see him until the afternoon. Glenda was obviously late and would surely arrive when he was having bedside chat with Holly.

'Hello darling, how are you feeling?' asked Holly as she greeted him with a peck on the cheek.

Spencer looked up at the entrance to the ward expecting Glenda to walk in any minute. He started to go hot, then cold and fidgeting all the time, wondering if his whole world would fall apart when Glenda walked through the door.

'Oh, I'm a little bit sore. I thought you were not coming to see me until the afternoon,' remarked Spencer and looking about him with concern expecting Glenda to appear at any moment.

'I couldn't do the afternoon, I have a hair appointment, so I have to leave here reasonably early,' said Holly.

Spencer's eyes were still trained on the ward doors. He mused that if Glenda walked in he would be in a right pickle. It was not as though in his weakened state that he could hide anywhere. He started to try to think of some excuses if this should happen, but couldn't think of anything that would sound convincing.

'You appear to be a bit edgy and you keep looking at the door. Are you expecting anyone?' asked Holly.

'Yes, I'm expecting a friend I work with,' replied Spencer as he continued to fidget in his bed.

'Anyway, I cannot stay long today, because as well as the hair appointment, I have some shopping to do,' said Holly.

The two of them chatted away for another ten minutes and then Holly made her excuses about the long return journey home she had to do and left. As she walked towards the door, she met Glenda entering the ward. The two women who were unknown to each other never even exchanged glances. Spencer was praying that Holly would not expose the problem of the two visiting partners by turning round and defining her departure with a blown kiss or a wave, but to Spencer's relief no goodbye gestures were made by her.

'Hello babe, I'm sorry I am late, the traffic has been terrible,' said Glenda as she came to the bedside, bent over towards him and gave a kiss.

'Oh, don't worry about being late, it's lovely to see you,' assured Spencer who thought that he had had a lucky escape and was now in a more relaxed mood.

Spencer realised that while he was in hospital danger lurked whenever visiting times came up. He told himself that he couldn't stay in hospital for any length of time in case one of them decided to change their visiting arrangements as Holly did. It was sheer luck that Spencer got away with it, but should it occur on another occasion, would he get away with it next time. In his thoughts he decided that he couldn't take that chance.

The man in the bed next to him was also becoming suspicious of the two different women that were visiting him and was beginning to find it quite amusing.

'Are you married?' asked his hospital neighbour in the adjacent bed.

'Yes, I'm afraid I am,' said Spencer not wishing to progress the conversation.

'Well then, who is the other woman? Is she your mistress?' asked the man.

'Yes, I suppose you could call her that. Now if you don't mind I'd like to have a little sleep,' replied Spencer as he turned over in his bed.

This diversionary measure prevented any further embarrassing questions from the patient next to him which Spencer was not happy to protract.

The remainder of the time Spencer spent in hospital went without incident and the two wives nominated by selection to visit, adopted Spencer's suggestion of seeing him at the times he had given them. The arrival of two different women being very affectionate towards the bed ridden invalid, caused much amusement throughout the ward and Spencer seemed to be the butt of the other patients jokes who never missed an opportunity to rib him on a daily basis. Over time, such was the hilarity at Spencer's expense, that he was pleased when the doctor gave him the official release from the hospital. He never wasted any time in informing his visiting wives that trips to the hospital were no longer necessary.

Having been released with a full medical bill of health, Spencer paid a visit to Iris who was not at all pleased that he had made no attempt to contact her after the accident.

'I thought you had done a runner and disappeared for good,' complained Iris.

'Well the reason I didn't contact you was that I had been in an accident. As you can see my arm is in plaster, having just been released from hospital,' pleaded Spencer.

'You could have let me know and I would have visited you,' protested Iris.

'I didn't want to worry you,' said Spencer.

'Worry me? I was worried sick. I tried your mobile phone, but it was turned off,' said Iris.

'Yes well, we are not allowed to use them in hospital, but don't concern yourself any longer, I'm here now,' replied Spencer who could see at the time that he was winning Iris over.

'What happens now about your treatment?' asked Iris.

'Well, I'm returning to hospital tomorrow to have this plaster cast removed and then I'm back on the road to catch up on some work I have missed out on,' replied Spencer.

Spencer stayed the night with Iris and true to his word he returned back to the hospital where he had the cast taken off and was back at work the same day.

Chapter 4 Promotion Offer

Spencer's employer was a man in his late fifties by the name of Gerald.   Everyone liked to call him Jerry.   He was a small man approximately five feet four inches in height, slim build and very well dressed.   Jerry afforded a certain affinity towards Spencer, thought he was a hard worker and knew that his faithful employee could always be relied upon to do anything asked of him.   It was one such day he was called into Jerry's office for further discussions about his future within the company.

'Spencer, you have been with us a number of years now and I know I can always trust you to do your best in the interests of this haulage company,' said Jerry.

'Thank you,' said Spencer who was lapping up the praise being dished out to him in large quantities.

'It is because of this that I would like to make you my new Transport Manager. As you know this is a job I have always done in the past and combined it with the General Manager's job, but I am getting too old for doing two jobs now, so I would like to pass on the Transport Manager's role to someone I can trust,' informed Jerry.

Without giving Spencer time to think about what he had said Jerry continued to spice up the offer.

'You will be given a company car with other emoluments which will compliment your new status, like an expense account and free fuel for your car, as well as a salary which will be approximately fifty percent higher than your current wage,' outlined Jerry with a broad smile over his face.

Before Spencer could even draw breath with a response, Jerry continued with more aspects about the position.

'You will therefore be no longer on the road, but instead report to this office every day and direct the tasks for the drivers on the payroll. Your new salary will be commensurate from the day that you start which will be next Monday,' continued Jerry still beaming away at the good news he was giving to Spencer.

Spencer listened to Jerry's office with intent and realised that as a married man this attractive job offer would have been perfect, but as a bigamist he would be working every day in the same place which did not suit his secret and varied lifestyle at all, in the way that constant travel did. The excuses he was currently making to his wives would no longer be a viable reason for staying away and they would all expect him to return home every night.

'I'm sorry Jerry, but I love the job I am doing and therefore are not looking to change it,' replied Spencer disheartened that his circumstances had forced him to reject the very attractive offer.

The smile immediately disappeared from Jerry's face. He was left stunned at such an attractive offer being turned down from his star employee.

'Alright Spencer you are a hard man to please. Instead of adding fifty per cent to your current wage I will give you double the money you are earning at present, together with a generous expense account,' said Jerry who was not ready to give up on seeing Spencer in the Job he wanted him to do.

Spencer was not happy that Jerry was making the offer more attractive and therefore increasingly difficult for him to refuse, but realised whatever inducements the boss put his way as an enticement would have to be refused.

'No Jerry, it's not the money. I'm just happy in the work that I am doing,' pressed Spencer.

'Alright then as you have turned it down, I will have to give the job to Jim. I'm sure he won't refuse it,' replied Jerry who appeared very disappointed that he hadn't won his prodigy over.

'No you can't offer the job to Jim Walker, that would be disastrous,' said Spencer who saw problems arising if he was his new boss.

'Sorry Spencer he is the only alternative who can do the job. If you don't want him to do it then you can still take the job yourself,' replied Jerry.

Spencer could see that Jerry was getting rather agitated about his interference and decided that it would be better to remain silent.

Now Jim was a difficult person to work with at the best of times and Spencer was aware that if he was made Transport Manager, then he could say goodbye to the easy working life he was currently enjoying.

What started off as an enjoyable chat with Jerry ended up as nightmare for Spencer, who visualised Jim in his mind wielding the big stick. Spencer was also upset that his own personal circumstances precluded him from taking the very attractive offer that was made. This was not concluded any better by the rejection of the offer, which made the boss displeased by Spencer's final decision.

Jim who was a largely built man in his mid thirties approximately six feet two inches in height and weighed approximately nineteen stone, had no hesitation in taking on the new role of Transport Manager offered by Jerry as predicted. Meanwhile, Spencer was aware that life under Jim's direction was not going to be easy.

The first job Spencer given under the new management was a run to Nice in the South of France. Spencer, who loathed anything over four hundred miles, knew that he just had to get on with it without any protests or gripes about the task. Jim would view a complaint as a reason to give out further unwelcome trips abroad and Spencer was aware of what the new Transport Manager was capable of doing. Spencer didn't like deliveries abroad because he was mindful that the wives would see even less of him than they do now. Holly was already complaining bitterly that she was left on her own too much.

Spencer, who never could agree with anything Jim did or say in the past, had to swallow his pride and do the best he could to get on the right side of his new boss. He just had to get on with it.

To make matters worse the journey to Nice was in the middle of July which was at the start of the School holiday season, making the main roads known as the autoroutes busier than usual, with long queues of traffic scattered intermittently between Paris and Lyons. Spencer loathed trips through France at this time of year, so in order to cut some time off his journey he made the decision not to stay overnight at Nice. After delivering his load he turned his vehicle round and headed back home. Two days after leaving Nice he arrived at Calais in the North West of France ready to cross the English Channel. By this time he was so tired that he never bothered to check his vehicle before boarding the ferry to Dover.

At Dover he was sectioned off by Border Control and his high sided vehicle searched. The rear doors of the lorry were opened by officials who noticed ten frightened looking Afghan citizens huddled together inside at the end of the vehicle, trying to shield their eyes from the sudden influx of light. The official came round to Spencer who was sitting in his cab waiting for the search to end and totally unaware that he was carrying other passengers.

'I'm sorry but I will have to hold you for questioning, you have been attempting to smuggle in illegal immigrants into this country,' said the official to Spencer.

Spencer was shocked by this revelation and blamed himself for not checking his vehicle before leaving Calais. His main problem was that he didn't know how long he was going to be held or even if the offence was serious enough to warrant a custodial sentence. He was asked by the official to inform his next of kin that he was being retained. He mused *'who should I phone Glenda? Iris? Holly? All three perhaps?'* Spencer didn't know what to do and decided eventually that he wouldn't tell any of them, but just remain a missing person for however long that would be.

After six agonising hours a Border Control official appeared and informed Spencer that he was lucky and could leave. Apparently the ten illegal immigrants admitted boarding Spencer's vehicle at Calais without his knowledge or permission. He dreaded informing the New Transport Manager of the error he had made in not making the mandatory checks on his vehicle before crossing the channel. Spencer thought it probably better not to say anything but blame his lateness on holiday traffic.

*

Life under the new management of big Jim was as Spencer expected, like a living hell. Jim, the new Transport Manager would contact Spencer any time night or day and provide him with a rota, which he would change many times over. If Spencer was in one end of the country Jim would issue work to him that would require travelling to the opposite end of the country. This played havoc with Spencer's home life, because there was nothing he could arrange with any certainty. Adding to his problems Spencer couldn't be certain that his unsociable work schedule was not being prepared to deliberately get him to leave the company, after all he and Jim were never great friends. Spencer thought it was time to speak to Jerry regarding the subject.

'Jerry, since you promoted Jim to be your new Transport Manager, I have had nothing but problems with my work schedule,' confided Spencer.

'What do you mean?' asked Jerry.

'Well, I appear to be doing a lot of travelling for very few deliveries,' reported Spencer.

'It's no good telling me things like that. The job of Transport Manager was offered to you and you turned it down,' replied a rather unsympathetic Jerry.

'What about the obvious wastage of fuel due to bad organisation,' pointed out Spencer.

Jerry appreciated that his driver's last remark was impacting on the profit of the business, and couldn't be left unchallenged.

'I'll have a word with him but I must advise you that I cannot interfere too much, after all he is managing the crews,' replied Jerry.

Jerry immediately walked into Jim's office. From the internal office window Spencer could see the two of them deep in conversation. Then Jim looked up and saw Spencer through the partition window. If looks could kill, then Spencer would be a dead man. Jerry then came out of Jims office and then Jim followed shortly afterwards and found Spencer.

'So you thought you would cross me did you by running to the boss with your little tittle tattle,' said a very angry Jim.

'I don't know what your game is Jim but the work you are giving me is counter productive and also not providing me with any home life,' remonstrated Spencer.

Jim grabbed Spencer by the collar with both hands.

'I'm warning you Andrews if you cross me again, then I will use my position in the company to get rid of you,' threatened Jim.

Spencer was placed in a difficult position. He could either comply with Jim's difficult style of management or risk getting sacked from a job he couldn't afford to lose.

Shortly after the argument with Jim, Spencer was sent on a French trip for a delivery in Nantes. Spencer disliked journeys abroad intensely and Jim knew it.

There was no problem dropping off the goods to their intended location, but on the way back there was some industrial action going on, with the French farmers blocking the sea ports. The result was that

Spencer was two days late reporting to Jim at the base, whereupon Jim saw this as a golden opportunity to sack him for his lateness.

Spencer, having received the letter went to see Jerry clutching in his hand the damning document.

'Jerry, do you know anything about this?' asked Spencer.

'I certainly do not,' replied Jerry, 'but follow me.' Jerry stormed off with the offending letter his hand, closely followed by Spencer.

The two of them marched into Jim's office, who was sitting relaxed reading a newspaper. As soon as he saw Jerry, like a naughty school boy Jim hid the newspaper under his desk.

'What is the meaning of this?' said Jerry throwing the letter on Jim's desk.

'Well it is because Spencer took a delivery to France and was two days late reporting back. We just can't tolerate that behaviour from drivers,' protested Jim.

'I agree, but in this case there were extenuating circumstances for his lateness. You must know that

Jim because you were reading the newspaper,' replied Jerry.

'Well it's not just that there have been other incidents,' remarked Jim.

'Listen to me. As far as I am concerned Spencer is a good worker, in fact one of the best, which is more than I can say for you Jim. Therefore he stays in this company, and your letter is withdrawn,' said Jerry tearing up the letter and throwing it into Jim's waste paper bin.

'Are you going above my authority?' protested Jim.

'As far as I am concerned you have no authority. You are sacked, you will receive a month's money in lieu of notice,' replied Jerry with venom in his voice.

Jim jumped up out of his chair banged the desk with his fist, but realising that his bad tempered display was not going to get him anywhere proceeded to clear his desk of his belongings.

Within a few minutes he had vacated the office and left the building.

'Now will you take the job of Transport Manager?' asked Jerry for the second time.

'No thank you Jerry. It's not a job I want to do,' replied Spencer knowing that he could never be assigned to a fixed work location for wives to locate him on a daily basis.

'Well I will be selecting one of the drivers then to take the post. Don't come running to me if the replacement is not to your liking,' warned Jerry.

Spencer shrugged his shoulders believing that whoever the replacement would be, he couldn't be worse than Jim.

In actual fact Jerry never did make a replacement, believing that he could do the job better than anyone he had working for him. Jerry having taken up his old role of Transport Manager, structured the tasks fairly to the workforce, much to Spencer's relief and satisfaction.

As far as Spencer was concerned life for him was back to normal and he could get back to keeping a well organised diary of visits to all his partners.

Chapter 5   Holly's Discontent

Spencer was taking a load to Blackpool from Birmingham when he received a call from Holly, his so-called second wife, on his mobile phone. The message was not a good one. Apparently she was complaining that he was not calling home enough. Also the money he was providing for her was insufficient and she wanted to end the marriage. This was terrible news as far as Spencer was concerned and he had to take the opportunity of turning into a road lay-by to recover from the shock.

The main problem for Spencer was that if she sought a divorce through the courts, there was a distinct possibility that he could be discovered as a bigamist, because in the eyes of the law Spencer's marriage to Holly was illegal. The theory being that a person cannot seek a divorce if he or she is not legally married in the first place. He had to get to Portsmouth immediately in an attempt to placate Holly and resolve the situation, but first he had to deliver his load in Blackpool and then drive southwards.

The drive South plagued Spencer's mind with the problems that could occur if Holly went ahead with her intentions. By the time he reached Portsmouth he was a nervous wreck and didn't relish the idea of confronting her.

Spencer entered the house with some trepidation and found Holly sitting in a chair in the lounge with her head in her hands.

'Now, Holly. What is all this silly talk about a divorce?' asked Spencer who tried to make light of the situation.

'It's not silly talk. I hardly ever see you,' remonstrated Holly.

'Are you serious about wanting this divorce?' asked Spencer.

'Yes, I am,' replied Holly, 'you leave me here alone to look after your child. The money you provide me with, is a mere pittance and insufficient for us to live on.'

Spencer realised through the brief conversation he had with Holly that the situation was more serious than he originally thought. However, he was now flush with money after his marriage to Iris, so he was at least able to remedy the financial situation.

'Look Holly, although I cannot do anything about spending more time with you because of my job, I am now doing a lot more overtime so I can give you more money,' said Spencer who was forlornly looking down at Holly sitting in the chair in her distressed state.

Holly didn't answer but looked up at him in some disbelief that he could suddenly pay her more after she had been struggling to pay the bills.

'In order to divorce me, you must have legitimate grounds, for example desertion, cruelty or adultery. No judge is going to grant a divorce to a woman whose husband is working all hours to provide for her,' argued Spencer. Holly pondered over Spencer's statement and then turned her attention towards him realising that he probably had a valid point.

'Oh yes, you are probably right. Perhaps I wasn't thinking straight. From the news that I received today, I wouldn't have dissolved the marriage anyway,' said Holly.

'Oh, and what news would that be?' asked Spencer, intrigued about what Holly was about to impart and why she had suddenly changed her mind.

'I'm expecting another child next November,' said Holly.

'Oh dear, I wasn't expecting that one coming,' replied the surprised Spencer.

'I expected you to be pleased about it Spencer,' said Holly in disgust over Spencer's apparent look of horror.

'I am, I am pleased about your news,' replied Spencer trying to hide his true feelings.

This was indeed a great shock for Spencer who realised that this would be his sixth child and viewed it as yet another mouth to feed and an additional expense. Spencer was numbed by the news and foolishly thought the answers to his problems could be eased if he drowned them in the local public house.

He gave Holly a quick peck on the cheek, told her that he wouldn't be long and headed off for some alcoholic comfort and sustenance. After entering the pub, he ordered himself a large beer and sat in the corner trying to dispel the problems that tortured his mind. He cut a lonely figure as he sat there deep in thought listening to all the local gossip that the regulars were passing between themselves. Some of the stories appeared quite captivating and in his efforts to crane his neck so that he didn't miss any of the local scandal, he didn't notice that another person had joined him at his table.

Suddenly he became aware that the person sitting at his table was a beautiful young woman approximately twenty seven years of age with red hair and brown eyes. In his loneliness he started to engage in conversation.

'It's unusual for a young woman to enter a public house on her own and order a drink,' said Spencer.

'Oh, I'm just waiting for my fiancé,' said the young woman who trained her eyes on the entrance door.

'You won't have to wait long. I think that is him walking over here now,' said Spencer.

'Yes, I see him,' she said as a broad smile came over her face.

A well dressed tall man with fair hair came over to the table, gave the girl a peck on the cheek and sat down at our table without ordering himself a drink.

It wasn't long before the conversation between the engaged couple had developed into a full scaled argument. Then they began shouting at one another exchanging insults, until the publican came over and asked the man to leave, which in his enraged state he was happy to do. He banged the table with his fist to illustrate his annoyance brushed past the publican almost knocking him over and stormed out of the door.

This brief episode of tantrums reduced the girl to tears. This was embarrassing for Spencer as he wasn't sure what he was to do, so he just sat there and pretended to ignore the girl's distress. Surprisingly she started to pour all her troubles out to him. Although Spencer didn't want to listen to her problems, he was forced to endure them nevertheless.

The tears continued to flow and the girl began to get quite hysterical which seemed to attract the attention of some of the other patrons in the pub. Their eyes were trained onto her as if they were going to witness more scenes of entertainment.

'Look, I think we had better get you home,' said Spencer believing that he had to stop the embarrassment of being the centre of attention by getting her out of the public house. Also he had started to feel sorry for the girl.

Spencer quickly finished his drink and walked the girl back to her house. On arrival Spencer said goodbye to the girl and turned round with the intention of making his way back to the Public House he had left.

'I can't thank you enough, you have been so good to me, please come in for a tea or coffee,' insisted the girl.

Spencer readily obliged and soon they were having cosy chats about anything and everything. As their conversation continued it wasn't long before Spencer had fallen into his usual style of chat up lines, which ended when they were exchanging names and telephone numbers. In the short time Spencer was in the house he had discovered that the girl was an accountant in a shareholder's office, her name was Janet and she owned the house she was living in. While they were indulging in cosy chats, Janet appeared to forget about the argument she had had with her fiancé. In not wishing to miss an opportunity which fell in line with his old habits, Spencer arranged a further day to meet up with Janet.

Holly thought that the threat of divorce to Spencer had done some good for she was now seeing a lot more of him. However the reality of the situation was that Spencer was in Portsmouth more often to see and spend time with his new found acquaintance Janet.

After a lapse of two months when he last saw Janet, Spencer was having a drink in his usual pub in Portsmouth when in walked Janet's fiancé. He saw Spencer and walked straight over to him. By the manner indicated by his body language he didn't appear to be too happy and replicated the mood he had when he last saw him.

'I thought I would find you in here,' said the man who displayed menacing anger.

'Oh, I remember you,' said Spencer. 'You were the person who arranged to meet a young lady in here and left after having an argument with her. As I remember the Publican asked you to leave.'

'I'm glad you remember me, because it didn't take you long to take advantage of the situation and start dating my fiancé,' said the man angrily as he moved his face in front of Spencer's.

Spencer could sense trouble brewing and tried to remonstrate with the man.

'How do you know all this?' asked Spencer.

'Don't worry, Janet has told me everything,' said the man who was clearly still very angry with Spencer.

'Well, I hope you are going to marry her, because if you don't you'll have me to deal with,' said the man.

'Why should I want to marry Janet,' Spencer argued, I just view her as a friend.

'Because she is also a good friend of mine and I don't want to see her get hurt any more,' said the man.

'That's not a good reason to marry her,' Spencer replied.

'It is if she was carrying your child,' said the man.

'And is she?' asked Spencer in shock.

'What do you think,' said the man emphasising the word 'you'.

'I'd better get round there right now and speak to her,' said Spencer.

'Yes, I think you better had,' insisted the man.

As Spencer left the pub the man shouted out.

'Remember what I said to you.'

With the words of Janet's fiancé ringing in his ears, Spencer went round to see Janet about the news he had just heard to see if it was genuine.

'It's real alright,' said Janet who was happy to see Spencer, 'I'm expecting the patter of tiny feet next March.'

'I've just been threatened by that fiancé of yours. He said if I didn't marry you, then he would deal with me. Whatever that meant,' said Spencer.

'You can forget about John, he is no longer my fiancé and therefore has no right to make such threats. If you decide to marry me, it will be because you want to,' said Janet.

Spencer could see that he was being pushed into another situation, but felt that he had no alternative. If Janet was carrying his child and he didn't want to let her down. However there was a nagging feeling in his mind that maybe the child could be John's after all they were going to get married. Spencer had to ask Janet the question.

'Janet are you sure that the child is not John's.'

'I am positive, I have never been intimate with John. He always wanted to wait until we were married,' replied Janet.

'Then in that case the child must be mine. Of course I will marry you,' Spencer blurted out believing that he had no alternative.

'Yes, you want to get married, but I don't even know your surname,' said Janet.

Spencer thought for a moment and said, 'The name is Drake, Spencer Drake.'

'Good, that's a nice name, I like it,' said Janet. 'As you are always on the road, I'll make the necessary wedding arrangements.'

'Just let me know what guests you would like me to invite,' continued Janet.

'No, I have no one to invite,' said Spencer.

'How strange,' said Janet puzzled by the reply, 'you must have family and friends you would like to see at the wedding.'

'I have no family and my friends live too far away and wouldn't want to make the journey,' replied Spencer.

Spencer's potential brides always asked the same questions prior to making the wedding arrangements, so he was always prepared with the stock set of answers.

Chapter 6   Family Problems

November came and so did the arrival of two more children born to Holly.   Holly who was only expected to deliver one child, unbeknown to her, she was carrying twins.   It seemed that Spencer must have been carrying the twin gene, because most of the births from his various wives were twins.   Again Spencer left the naming of the twins to Holly who called the two boys Richard and Stanley.

Time was overdue for Spencer to see his third wife Iris in Torbay, Devonshire.   He thought that if he was to get as far away from Portsmouth as he could his troubles would be over.

This however proved incorrect, because when he reached Iris he was informed that she also was expecting twins also due in March.   It seemed wherever Spencer went, trouble was never far behind him.   However Spencer realised that in marrying the wealthy Iris, money ceased to become a problem and was a useful asset in sustaining his large and ever increasing brood spread throughout the United Kingdom.

Now Spencer had parents who lived in Dawlish which is in the same county Devonshire, who he hadn't seen in some time and decided that while he was visiting Iris he might as well call on his mother and father.

Both parents were delighted to see Spencer especially his mother who doted on him and spoilt him as a child.

'Spencer. Isn't it about time you took an interest in girls and got yourself married,' said his mother.

'Plenty of time for that, mum,' said Spencer who had no wish to continue with this line of questioning.

'No, I can't agree with you Spencer, you are now in your mid thirties and time is passing you by,' said his mother.

'Why do you want to marry me off?' asked Spencer, 'I'm perfectly happy as I am.'

'One thing your father and I always wanted was a few grandchildren,' said his mother.

'Look mother you know how I feel about marriage,' protested Spencer.

'Oh, I'm well aware of that. You also seem to shy away from women,' replied his mother.

'I sometimes think you know me too well,' said Spencer, who was tiring of the awkward and difficult conversation which required a lot of thought before making his replies.

'You're missing out on a valuable part of life,' argued his mother.

'No mother, I'm afraid that this family thing is not for me. Anyway, how would I look after them. I'm always on the road,' remonstrated Spencer.

'Spencer you are our only child and it sounds as though you are going to deny your father and I our only wish. When you are older, you will live to regret not getting married and having a family of your own,' said Spencer's mother.

'Look mother, that is enough talk about marriage, family life and the like. It's not for me and let there be an end to this conversation,' replied Spencer who was becoming exasperated with his mother.

Spencer decided that he was getting enough grief with all the persistent questions and advice on all the benefits of a family life and decided to make a hasty retreat back to his third wife Iris. On the short journey back he pondered over the conversation he had had with his parents and the lies he was forced to make in order to cover his guilty secret. *'If only they knew, they could become very poor people if they were to buy Christmas and Birthday presents to the many daughter in laws and grandchildren to which they were in complete oblivion.'*

The month of March soon came round and brought additional problems for Spencer. Iris produced the twins expected which was a boy and a girl who were called Thomas and Ursula and Janet who he was yet to marry, produced a girl called Vera.

April was selected as the month he was to marry Janet at Portsmouth. This was a church wedding and the pews were packed with Janet's relations and friends, although as expected there was no one from Spencer's side to witness the happy event. In this case Janet who had already had the child, was walking up the aisle without a lump in front of her. This made a change for Spencer who amongst his other wives, most of which were pregnant for the ceremony.

During the ceremony the priest raised the usual question to the assembly 'Does any person here present know any just cause or impediment why these two should not be joined in holy matrimony, let him now speak or forever hold his peace.'

Spencer's heart missed a few beats pending the pause which followed the question and was relieved when no one answered. The next problem he had to face was when he left the church, because there was a possibility that the wedding would attract some of the townspeople who may have been shopping that day, but wanted a glimpse of the brides outfit. If his second wife Holly who lived in Portsmouth happened to be one of those spectators, Spencer could have been in deep trouble. On leaving the church, sure enough a crowd had gathered as expected. Spencer's eyes were scanning every onlooker. He was also ready to make a quick dart to safety should either Holly or Holly's parents be amongst those that had gathered.

Life was now becoming really complex for Spencer who now had four wives and ten children. Remembering their names and who was included in each family, was a task in itself. In fact he had to write down all the different surnames he had used to marry his wives and the names of all his many children. He would leave this list in the cab of his lorry and practice the names of the family he was due to visit. Also a new wife meant he had less time to afford on the other spouses. Added to which, Iris his third wife was totally unaware that she was contributing to the living expenses of all his families.

Spencer realising the seriousness of the situation he had created for himself, would often go off alone to a park or a wood where he could enjoy complete solitude, without having to worry about mistakes in coming out with the wrong names to his children and wives.

It was on one such day that Spencer was in Birmingham walking through the local park when he found himself a seat and just watched the world go by. He never took Glenda on such walks because that would have meant bringing also the four children. He loved the solitude and children happily playing around him would not afford him the peace and quietness that he craved. However, maybe on this particular day he may have wished that he had brought his Birmingham family along.

A female jogger of slim build approximately five feet four inches in height with brown hair and blue eyes ran passed Spencer's seat, stopped turned around and sat on the bench seat next to him puffing and panting with exhaustion. Spencer remained silent believing that if he didn't speak he would not get involved with this girl.

'That's better,' she said after getting her breath back.

Spencer didn't comment.

'Do you do any jogging,' said the girl to Spencer.

'No, I'm afraid I don't. Maybe I should try and get myself fit, I certainly need it,' said Spencer.

'You look as though you could do with a bit of fitness regime. Well there is nothing like the present, come on get up and I'll race you down to the park cafe,' said the girl.

Spencer thought that this was an odd person who would happily talk to strangers and get them involved in the things that she liked doing. He did what he was asked to do, but was no match for the girl who reached the park cafe first and waited for him to arrive. When Spencer did eventually arrive at the cafe, he was puffing and panting, needing support of the wall to regain his breath and almost fell over with exhaustion.

'You are definitely not fit. Come on I'll treat you to a cup of tea in the cafe,' said the girl.

Spencer again found it strange that this person, whom he didn't know, offered to buy him a drink. He staggered puffing and panting through the cafe doors and flopped onto a chair at the nearest table to the cafe entrance.

'Gosh,' he said recovering to his normal breathing, 'I'll need a bit more practice before I do that again. That was really full on.'

The girl came over with the teas and sat opposite Spencer.

'Now,' she said, 'my name is Karen and who are you.'

'Why do you want to know my name, I've only just met you?' asked a puzzled Spencer.

'Look. If I'm buying someone I haven't met before a tea, I really ought to know who I'm buying it for,' said Karen.

This was normally the standard patter that Spencer came out with, but in this situation the roles had been reversed.

'I suppose you're right. I'm Spencer.'

'Right then Spencer, I would like to be your lover, so you had better get in shape. That means losing a little bit of that stomach,' said Karen patting his waste level.

Spencer almost choked on his tea. He had never been propositioned by a woman before in this forthright manner, which appeared to exclude all shame. It was always him who made the first move, but whenever he did, it was never as quite direct as the way Karen had just approached him.

'That's rather direct Karen. Oh, I don't think that's a very good idea, do you?' said Spencer determined not to get involved with another woman.

'Since you ask the question, I think it's an excellent idea,' said Karen not at all phased by her cheeky approach.

'But you don't know anything about me, I could even be married,' said Spencer.

'No! Not you. You don't look the marrying type,' said Karen.

'Why do you say that?' asked Spencer.

'Well look at you. Your shirt doesn't look as though it has been ironed and you don't wear a wedding ring. No! You're not married,' said Karen convinced that from her observations that she was right.

Spencer let Karen believe her conclusions of him and never made any attempt to correct her.

'Thank you for the tea anyway,' said Spencer who changed the subject and was still determined not to get involved.

'Come on, hurry up drinking that tea, I have some more exercise in mind for you,' said Karen.

Spencer naively thought that Karen was enticing him into a bit more running and dutifully obliged. As soon as they left the cafe, Karen commenced running slowly and then quickened up into a sprint. Spencer in the meantime had a job to keep up.

Karen led Spencer back to her house where Spencer who again was puffing and panting was invited inside. In the lounge she wasted no time in stripping off her clothes, including Spencer's and indulging in wild passionate love making.

'I said you would enjoy that,' commented Karen.

'Yes, you were right,' said Spencer.

'Right, we will meet here in a week's time and repeat the experience,' said Karen determined that Spencer should return to see her.

It appeared that Karen was dictating dates to suit her calendar and even the agenda of what they were going to do when they meet up.

'I can't do that, it will have to be in two month's time, because I'm always on the road,' said Spencer.

'Okay, two months it is, but make sure you turn up,' insisted Karen.

Two months later, Spencer returned to Karen's house only to discover that Karen was pregnant.

'I suppose it's a silly question to ask if the child is mine,' said Spencer.

'You're right it is a silly question and also an insulting one. Of course the baby inside me is yours, stupid,' said Karen.

'You told me that you had taken protection,' said Spencer.

'Well, I lied to you, only because I always wanted a child,' said Karen.

'That was not a nice thing to do. You shouldn't have done that. I hardly knew you at the time,' replied Spencer.

'Well, you knew me enough to jump into bed with me,' said Karen.

'I thought it was just for a bit of fun. How wrong I was,' said Spencer.

'You will have to marry me now in order to regularise the situation,' insisted Karen who was never backward in coming forwards.

'Regularise the situation? Oh, I don't know about that,' replied Spencer.

'I do,' said Karen, 'My father is in the next room. Would you like me to get him so that you can have a little chat with him?' said Karen.

Spencer realised that he was again placed in a difficult situation and didn't want to explain to other members of Karen's family, the circumstances that resulted in her pregnancy. That would have been most embarrassing.

'No, that won't be necessary. Of course I'll marry you. As you are pregnant we will have to get married,' Spencer finally agreed.

'Good I knew you would do the decent thing and not leave me to bring this child up on my own,' said Karen

'Right that's settled then. I'll leave you to make all the arrangements,' confirmed Spencer.

Spencer rolled these words off the tongue without the slightest thought of the consequences. It was as if he was used to coming out with this life changing statement.

'By the way. What is your surname?' asked Karen.

'Spencer had to think before giving his answer, 'It's Evans, Spencer Evans,' said Spencer.

'Well, Spencer Evans come back to Birmingham in three months time wearing a nice suit and I'll have all the arrangements sorted out,' insisted Karen.

Spencer then realised that he had been well and truly trapped. It appeared that Karen had planned the whole thing. She was looking for a husband and a child and had managed successfully to get the child and lure a reluctant Spencer into marriage as part of her carefully conceived plan. The ease with which she achieved this surprised her closest friends and family who were anxious to meet the person who had succumbed so easily to Karen's will.

When the three months had elapsed, Spencer received a call on his mobile phone to make himself available for the wedding, which he duly did like a lamb to the slaughter.

Spencer was getting so used to these wedding ceremonies that he had got everything off to a fine art. The groom's speech, he had done so often that he could recite it word verbatim without looking at his notes. He was also well versed at greeting guests. Karen Evans had become Spencer's fifth wife.

The guests appeared to be happy and relaxed in conversation when Karen came over to Spencer and gently grabbing his arm.

'Come on, I want you to meet my brother. He has just arrived, unfortunately because of traffic jams he missed the wedding ceremony, but at least he has not missed the reception,' said Karen.

Spencer was dragged by the arm through a crowd of guests.

'There he is over there,' said Karen.

As Spencer approached nearer to the brother Karen wanted him to meet, Spencer got the shock of his life. It was Jim Walker, the Transport Manager who was sacked from Spencer's firm of hauliers.

'Not you again,' said Jim to Spencer, who then turned his attention on Karen.

'This man was instrumental in me losing my job,' said Jim to Karen.

'I'm sure you must be exaggerating,' replied Karen.

'I most certainly am not. How can you marry a man like him?' asked Jim.

'Not now Jim. Just enjoy the evening,' replied Karen.

'Anyway I thought you were already married,' said Jim to Spencer.

'Don't be silly Jim. How could he be married when he has just married me?' intervened Karen.

'Okay, I must be thinking of one of the other drivers, but I was sure it was you,' said Jim.

Jim leant over and whispered discretely in Spencer's ear out of hearing range of Karen.

'I don't like you. Never did like you. Just keep out of my way.'

Spencer made no comment but left Jim to contemplate his anger while he mingled with other guests. However, it seemed wherever he went in the room, Jim was there looking at him.

The wedding appeared to go well and Spencer settled down once again to married life.

So time went by and Spencer's eleventh child was borne to Karen, a boy who she called William. As for Spencer he merely added the additional name to the families list he was keeping in his cab.

Chapter 7 The Test

Spencer was not in the best of moods and was concerned about how he was going to overcome his busy schedule for the day, so he set off two hours earlier than he had originally intended.

A visit to Great Yarmouth on the coast of Norfolk to pick up some rod reinforcement was on Spencer's list for jobs to be done in the day. He arrived early. As the yard was locked up he was unable to access it to load up his goods. He decided to look around the market pending waiting for someone to arrive to unlock the premises. He thought he might be able to kill some time before returning to arrange the pick up his load. After an hour of walking around stalls that did not attract any interest, which mainly consisted of women's clothes and jewellery he found himself a bench seat away from the hustle and bustle and sat down.

He hadn't rested himself long, when a slim attractive woman approximately aged thirty with dark long hair sat beside him. Wearing a short skirt, she didn't seem to mind showing off her shapely long legs. Spencer resigned himself not to converse with her in any shape, form or otherwise. In fact he adopted a bolt upright sitting pose looking straight ahead of him, not daring to move a muscle. His eyes were directed anywhere in the square other than on the woman sitting next to him.

'It's tiring walking around the market. I saw you walking round the stalls earlier,' the woman said to Spencer.

Spencer didn't answer her, but still retained his bolt upright pose and made no eye contact.

The woman, realising that she was not going to get an answer from Spencer, looked intensely at him wondering why he had remained mute. She then looked away in disbelief, stared back at him as if she had just witnessed an alien dropping to earth. Then her curiosity got the better of her.

'Hello! Hello! Are you foreign or something?' asked the woman snapping her fingers at him in order to get his attention.

'Look, I never asked you to sit on this bench seat and I never asked you to talk to me,' said Spencer, which were the words used on him when he first met Glenda.

'Are, at least I've got you talking to me. And you are not foreign after all, I was beginning to think you either couldn't understand me or were dumb, deaf or just plain stupid,' said the woman.

'Well as you can see I am none of those things you've mentioned,' replied Spencer.

'Look, my names Rachael. So let's start again. What's your name?' asked the woman stretching out her hand for a handshake.

Spencer reluctantly offered his hand. He couldn't believe it. This woman had given her name without him even asking for it. This person, who called herself Rachael, was trying to pick him up and exacting the same tactics as he used to adopt.

'They call me Spencer,' he said still adopting his same uncomfortable posture.

Spencer turned his head to look at her. She was stunning sitting cross legged in her bright yellow dress. He looked briefly away thinking about the promise he had made to himself and then directed his eyes back at her. Spencer then decided that nothing could be gained by continuing his rude behaviour towards this woman.

'Rachael, it is very nice to meet you, but shouldn't you be getting back to your husband?' enquired Spencer.

'Oh, I'm not married, and never have been married,' Rachael replied with confidence and smiling.

Spencer started to think that it was a terrible situation he had been placed in, talking to a beautiful single girl. He was aware of the danger warning lights signalling in his mind and told himself that this woman had to be avoided at all costs. One thing he didn't want to do was repeat the many mistakes he had made in the past.

'No you may not be married, but I am and I think my wife would be very jealous if she knew I was talking to a beautiful woman like you,' remarked Spencer with a grin.

'Well, she is not here, so how would she know that,' replied Rachael who seemed to be tantalising close to flirting with Spencer.

'Because I would have no hesitation in telling her,' said Spencer applying the immediate brush off.

'Do you tell your wife everything? I mean all you are doing this morning is walking around the market, then sitting on a bench seat talking to someone,' commented Rachael.

Spencer thought about the question. Normally his life is surrounded with lies, deceit and trying to cover up his tracks. The way that Rachael had put the question followed by a comment sounded quite ordinary and innocuous.

'No. I wish I had the courage to tell them everything,' said Spencer immersed in thought.

'Them? How many wives have you got?' asked Rachael with a laugh.

Spencer realised that he had made a verbal blunder and immediately tried to rectify it.

'Them? Did I say them? I mean her. A slight slip of the tongue,' said Spencer who didn't want to enlarge on his mistake.

'Oh, I do think that's funny. For a brief moment I'd got the distinct impression that you had a harem of wives,' said Rachael who was still laughing. 'I can just imagine you running around trying to share your time between your harem.'

'Oh, that's very funny. Now why would I want several wives? One is enough,' said Spencer who was trying to be convincing by continuing to chuckle along with Rachael about the conversation.

'It's me poking fun at you, although I shouldn't tease you like this,' said Rachael who had by then, really got a bad attack of the giggles.

'You seem to find that funny, but tell me. Do you think the law should be changed in this country in favour of men marrying more than one wife?' asked Spencer.

'What a strange question. No I don't, and I don't agree with it. Anyone that tries to marry another partner and think that he or she can get away with it, should suffer the full penalties that the law can impose,' replied Rachael.

'Interesting that you should think like that,' said Spencer who was deep in thought.

'As you have raised the question, what do you think?' enquired Rachael.

'Oh, I have no defining view on it,' replied Spencer, who was trying to release himself from a difficult situation.

Spencer was beginning to find himself drawing towards this girl. She had all the attributes that he liked about a woman, a pretty face, a nice figure and above all, a sense of humour. However he was sensible enough to realise that he couldn't succumb to her charms, so he started to think of an excuse to find a way out of the situation. He began looking at his watch.

'Gosh is that the time? It's ten minutes past nine o'clock,' remarked Spencer.

'Well, it's been nice meeting you Rachael, I really must get away. I have a lot to do today,' said Spencer who continued to laugh with Rachael. However he wasn't amused about the same thing that Rachael saw so funny. Spencer was laughing at the fact that Rachael was not aware of his true circumstances, meaning that he hadn't made a slip of the tongue at all.

Spencer rose from his chair smiled at Rachael, walked swiftly down the road until he was out of her view, jumped high above the pavement and punched the air with his fist.

'Yes, I've cracked it,' he yelled with delight. Spencer mused that he had turned his back on temptation and passed the test of rejecting beautiful women with flying colours. He appeared so pleased with himself as if he had passed a difficult examination, which in essence he really had.

However, what he found so puzzling was that in his single days he used to be the pursuer, which required a silver tongue and well rehearsed chat up lines in order to date a woman. Now he is married several times over, he discovered that the roles had been reversed. In fact the predictable 'chat up' lines are being played back to him by the opposite sex. In his egoistic mind he felt that Rachael was not up to his standard of 'chat up' and needed a bit more practise. He confessed to himself that he found her style a bit predictable and not very original.

Spencer continued the day in a cheery mood believing that he had overcome his weakness of trying to date every beautiful woman that came within distance of his eye view. He started to think of it as an illness, for which he was well on the way to recovery. Spencer considered that he was a player no longer and walked through Great Yarmouth towards his lorry with his head held high. On the way he passed several beautiful woman whom he would give a brief sideway's glance and continued without stopping or breaking stride in his step. This was indeed a changed man, who had faced and overcome his greatest problem of serial dating arising from any daily temptation put to his disposal.

Chapter 8 The Wives at Birmingham

Six months elapsed since William was born to Karen and Spencer had arranged that he would call in to see her. He also arranged a visit to Glenda. Spencer drove into Birmingham and called into a supermarket to buy cigarettes and a newspaper. As he walked in the door he saw Glenda with the two sets of twins, talking to a woman with a young child. He was about to approach her when he realised that the woman she was talking to was Karen. Spencer immediately stopped in his tracks.

Luckily for Spencer he wasn't seen by either of the two women or the children, so he quickly retraced his steps out of the supermarket and went straight home to Glenda's house and let himself in. He then sat in an armchair waiting for Glenda's arrival.

When Glenda did eventually walk into the house, she was full of gleeful chat.

'Hi Spencer,' said Glenda as she came over and gave him a kiss. 'Guess who I saw today.'

'I can't imagine,' said Spencer.

'It was Karen, an old school friend who I haven't seen for years. I know that you are not familiar with the name, but she is really a very nice person. She has a little boy by the name of William,' said Glenda brimming over with excitement.

'Does she live near here?' asked Spencer as he pondered a method of attempting to end the conversation.

'No! Not too far. In fact we have arranged to keep in touch. However, listen to this. Karen also has a husband called Spencer and even more coincidental, he also is a lorry driver. Like me, she doesn't see much of him either. Nevertheless we thought it might be a good idea if we met each other's husbands,' said Glenda excited about the prospect of a foursome get-together. 'So darling you let me know when you're next at home and I will arrange us all to meet up. Her husband and you, both being in the same type of work and would have a lot in common to talk about.'

'I'm sure I'd love to meet both of them, but you must be aware that with my job I can't plan anything and I'm certain Karen's husband, would be exactly the same,' replied Spencer.

'Well alright it would be nice if you could just meet her. Tell you what, I'll arrange it next time you are home,' said Glenda.

'Okay, you do that,' answered Spencer. 'Right, I have to go out now and get some cigarettes.'

Spencer was happy to leave the house to release himself of the difficult conversation he was having with Glenda and headed straight to his other home in Birmingham, where Karen lived.

When he arrived Karen had just finished her shopping and couldn't wait to tell Spencer about the old school friend called Glenda who she had met. She was equally excited about seeing her again.

'Do you know, the poor woman has two sets of twins. I don't know how she copes,' said Karen.

'Yes it must be really hard on her,' agreed Spencer feeling uncomfortable about the conversation.

'Her husband is also called Spencer, which is a real coincidence. Spencer, being such an unusual name. We have agreed that we will all meet up,' said Karen.

'Oh, that's nice,' said Spencer.

'Look babe, I'm afraid this is only a fleeting visit today, because I have to be back on the road,' said Spencer. With that, Spencer gave Karen a quick peck on the cheek, said goodbye to young William and returned back to Glenda's house.

The following day, Spencer was back on the road heading towards Southampton. On the drive towards the south coast he started to muse over the events that occurred the day before and how to resolve what appeared to be a difficult situation. In his wildest dreams, he never imagined that two of his wives would ever meet up, particularly in a large town like Birmingham and form what appeared to be a lasting friendship. Worst of all try and arrange a meeting with the husbands involved, both of whom happened to be him. He thought that if this situation was played out in a television sit-com, people would find in very amusing, however as it was reality, it wasn't funny at all and needed careful planning involving a strategy of evasion.

Spencer had arranged that while he was in Southampton he would visit Portsmouth and call in on Holly and Janet. Although Spencer liked visiting his wives he dreaded any bad news that they wished to impart. Bad news always seemed to centre round new additions to his ever expanding brood. He didn't know which wife was going to make an announcement to him next.

As Spencer approached the house he saw Janet in the front garden playing with little Vera.

'Hello darling,' he greeted and went straight over and gave her a kiss.

'And how are you little one,' he said picking three year old Vera up and giving her a hug.

'I've had a bit of an arduous journey, so I hope you haven't got any bad news for me,' said Spencer.

'No,' said Janet, 'only good news. I'm going to be a mother again.'

Spencer's face dropped. Hardly believing what was said to him.

'Oh, that's wonderful news,' replied Spencer as he did his best to hide his true feelings.

Spencer was wondering how he was going to cope with all this additional expense. He was already raiding Iris's account, drawing out large amounts of money and doing as much overtime as he could get.

However, the eleven children he already had plus one on the way was, only part of his problems. He was beginning to see lovemaking as a chore. As he was dividing his time amongst five wives, each one saw him very sporadically, so they had to make the most of the short time they were with him. Spencer was becoming very tired and losing a lot of weight in trying to satisfy the sexual demands of his wives, together with any running repairs that had to be done in the houses during the course of the visits. Also in attempting to maintain complete secrecy from the wives, he had to be careful what he said whenever he was in their company. One innocent slip of the tongue could expose his bigamist activities. There were also the telephone calls which created the largest problem, because sometimes he would receive these on his mobile phone whilst in the company of one of the wives. Also whilst on the telephone, he should ask who was speaking and the caller answered 'your wife,' then if he didn't recognise the voice, he quickly had to ascertain the identity of the caller.

One such call he received from Glenda. Her Birmingham accent was very similar to Karen's and Spencer made the mistake of calling her 'Karen'.

This was the first time he had ever slipped up on names. Glenda immediately picked up on the error.

'Karen? Why are you calling me Karen, that is the name of my friend?' said Glenda.

Spencer realising his mistake, quickly tried to retrieve the situation.

'Oh I'm sorry Glenda, I thought you were Karen the girl who works in the office. Anyway why do you want to speak to me?' asked Spencer.

'I just want to let you be aware that Karen, not the Karen you know, will be visiting me tomorrow and I would like you to be there to meet her. She will also try to get hold of her husband in an attempt to get him to come along. I will arrange a child sitter and maybe we can all go out to lunch' said Glenda.

'I'm sorry babe but I am working tomorrow,' replied Spencer, who although available had no alternative than to make an excuse.

'This always happens when I try and arrange something with you involved. Oh never mind I shall invite them around just the same,' said Glenda.

Spencer was becoming very uneasy about the relationship the two wives had developed between them. They seemed to be getting too friendly with each other which could only spell out 'trouble'. He decided that he would limit the time he spent at Birmingham. He had to ensure that whenever he did arrange to meet up with either Glenda or Karen that he was not going to be disturbed by an unwelcome alternative wifely caller.

The following day Karen appeared on Glenda's doorstep as arranged.

'Where's your husband?' asked Glenda, 'I thought you were going to bring him with you.'

'He is working today, and I couldn't persuade him. I tried really hard,' said Karen.

'Please come in,' said Glenda, 'and make yourself at home.'

Karen walked in with her three year old son William and sat herself on one of the lounge chairs.

By this time Glenda's two sets of twins, who were eight years of age and ten, were running around making a hell of a racket. They were knocking things over and generally being aggravating little monsters. Glenda had the solution to the problem.

'Right you four can go out into the garden and take William with you, also make sure you look after him,' said Glenda.

The two women having rid themselves of the noisy playful antics of the children, started to talk about the times they were at school together and seemed to be getting on fine and enjoying each others company. They laughed a lot in the cause of reminiscing over the past, sipping large glasses of wine in the process, occasionally taking it in turns to check on the children.

Then Karen's attention was drawn to some photographs on the other side of the lounge. She left her chair, walked over to the mantle piece and looked closely at one of the photo's which graced the room. Her eyes were straining as she looked at the man in the photograph, which was a striking resemblance to her husband.

'Why did you have a photograph taken with my husband?' asked Karen perturbed at what she had just seen and taking another look just to make certain.

'No, you must be mistaken Karen, that is my husband,' insisted Glenda.

'I don't think so, I'd recognise him anywhere, also that suit and tie I have seen many times before,' remarked Karen.

Glenda immediately became pale with shock, partly doubting and not wanting to believe what Karen was saying.

'Are you thinking what I am thinking,' said Glenda.

'Yes, as incredible as it seems I do think I am, although I don't want to believe what I'm thinking,' replied Karen.

'Do you think Spencer has married both of us?' asked Glenda.

The two women looked at one another in shocked silence, not quite understanding what was unfolding before their eyes.

'No he wouldn't have done, would he? Although there is a distinct possibility that he may have,' replied Karen.

'No surely not,' said Glenda as doubt started to re-appear in her mind.

The two women looked at one another in stark amazement.

'Look there is only one way to settle this. Have you got any wedding photographs?' asked Karen.

'Yes, I have and I shall get them,' replied Glenda.

Glenda left the room and returned with a wedding album. The two women poured over the photographs. Karen was quick to pick out obvious similarities, for example shoes, suit and tie.

'The cheeky devil, he married me in the same suit that he married you,' said Karen.

'Are you sure?' asked Glenda.

'That is definitely the man I married, and unless he has an identical twin who wears the same clothes, there is no doubt in my mind whatsoever. Also using the same name is a complete giveaway,' said Karen.

'Oh dear, we've been such fools,' said Glenda.

'I know,' said Karen, 'but not any more. It's time we played a game on our Spencer and taught him a lesson, he won't forget in a hurry.'

'You're right, I've got an idea. I'll give him a call,' said Glenda as she picks up the phone.

'Hello darling, it's Glenda here, when will you next be coming home.'

'I will be there in two days time, perhaps you can arrange for a child sitter so that I can take you out for a meal,' said Spencer.

'That sounds nice. That will be Wednesday. Where were you thinking of going,' asked Glenda.

'Well, I thought we could try that new bistro called Bridges,' said Spencer.

'Alright give me a time and I will book it,' said Glenda.

'Let's say half past seven,' confirmed Spencer.

'Okay, darling looking forward to seeing you,' said Glenda and gently put the phone down.

'It's perfect. That's it Karen, be in Bridges Bistro in two days time. A good time to arrive will be eight o'clock. It will then, that we will put our sting into operation,' said Glenda.

Wednesday evening arrived and so did Spencer who was totally unaware that his evening was going to be a complete devastation and a day he would never forget.

'Come on,' said Glenda urging her husband to hurry up, 'the table is booked, so we don't want to be late.'

Spencer was keen to oblige to his wife's demands to rush about, because he didn't want to stay in the house too long, in case Karen made an unscheduled call.

In the restaurant Spencer ordered the starter meals for Glenda and himself and settled down in the friendly ambience of the restaurant, happily chatting away to Glenda and totally unaware of the memorable experience which was about to unfold before his very eyes.

At eight o'clock prompt, in walked Karen as scheduled. Spencer had his back to the restaurant door so he did not see her arrival. As Karen walked towards the couple's table she winked at Glenda which was acknowledged with a very discrete wave of the hand which Spencer did not see. The actors in place, were ready to give the best performance of their lives.

'Oh hello, fancy seeing you here,' said Glenda greeting Karen. Karen by this time had walked behind Spencer.

Spencer who was aware that Glenda had welcomed someone, although didn't even turn his head to see who the person was, but happily continued eating his starter completely oblivious to the presence of Karen. Glenda thought it was time that the sting was kick started into action with some introductions. Glenda immediately addressed Spencer.

'Spencer this is my dear friend Karen who I spoke to you about,' said Glenda to Karen who was standing behind Spencer.

Spencer quickly turned his head to look at the new arrival and almost choked on his food with shock. He was mortified and dumbstruck at the spectacle of seeing Karen and Glenda in the same room. Karen who wanted to make the most of the situation continued with the play acting along with her friend.

'Hello darling,' she said as she came over and kissed him.

'Do you two know one another?' said Glenda who had then got well into her role.

'I should hope so, he's my husband,' said Karen, 'but what is he doing taking you out to dinner? If he takes any woman out to dinner it should be me.'

'He can't be your husband, because he is my husband,' said Glenda adopting a puzzled look.

Spencer was getting more and more uncomfortable as the well rehearsed conversation between the two women progressed. At this moment, Spencer wished that the floor would open up and swallow him. The one place he didn't want to be, was in that restaurant at that moment with two curious wives. The embarrassment of the situation was overwhelming. Listening to the two women arguing on the subject of whom he belonged, caused his face to redden up and sweat roll down the back of his neck. Karen whose mood had now changed to anger turned her attention to Spencer.

'So, who are you married to? Tell this silly woman once and for all, because I think she is a bit confused,' insisted Karen.

'I'm married to both of you,' said Spencer in his agitated state. This was the first time he had revealed his secret, although he hoped that if he ever was forced to make this exposure it would not be in front of a crowded restaurant. Also he hoped if ever the situation did arrive he would at least have been able to fully prepare himself for the eventuality.

'You can't be,' insisted Glenda, 'that's against the law. Isn't it?'

Spencer didn't know where to put himself and unusually for him he was lost with an answer but in this instance thought it more prudent not to answer Glenda's question.

By this time many of the patrons in the restaurant had stopped eating as they were more interested in this rather strange conversation that was taking place in their midst. Some were giggling, pointing or whispering amongst themselves. Spencer's degradation was now complete and the two wives realised that they had done what they had set out to do. The sting went as planned to perfection exacting maximum embarrassment to the victim. Spencer wanted to remove himself and his two wives from the restaurant and avoid the entertainment he was providing to the diners. The three were also subjected to odd comments that induced raucous laughter from their appreciative audience.

'Can we go home and I will tell you everything, but I can't talk about it here in front of everyone in the restaurant. People are listening and making fun of us,' said Spencer.

'Where's home, it appears you have two homes,' said Karen who realised that she now had a star role in her acting, as she played along with those who were enjoying the entertainment.

The diners in the restaurant gave a rapturous applause to this remark as well as a few hoots and laughs as if they were watching a London West End show.

'We will go back to Glenda's house,' confirmed Spencer, who not wishing to stay longer than he had to, quickly paid the dinner bill and left ushering the two women out the door in the process. When they had gone, the restaurant erupted in a noisy laughter which could be heard outside. This angered Spencer as he made his way to his car.

Back at Glenda's house the saga continued. Spencer was once again put in the spotlight and overcome with embarrassment as he battled with the barrage of difficult questions that were put to him.

'So what made you marry two women,' asked Glenda who was anxious to get straight to the point.

'Well, I didn't intend it. Karen initially did all the running. In response I tried to ignore her advances,' said Spencer.

'But you didn't, did you? In the end you made me pregnant,' said Karen who wasn't going to be blamed for Spencer's failings.

'Karen suggested marriage having found that she was expecting a child and threatened to involve her father if I didn't marry her,' said Spencer.

'Involve my father? I think we ought to involve the police, don't you Glenda?' said Karen who was not convinced by Spencer's explanation or excuses. Spencer didn't wait for Glenda's answer.

'No! Don't do that. They will put me away for a long time,' pleaded a nervous and shocked Spencer.

'Give us one good reason why we shouldn't tell the police everything we know, after all you have committed bigamy, adultery and goodness knows what else,' said Glenda, who after a bit of play acting was beginning to leave her star role and return to the seriousness of the situation.

'If I go to prison, then I will be unable to financially look after you or Karen or the children,' said a discontented Spencer.

Glenda realising that Spencer had made a valid point nodded apprehensively in agreement.

'Well from my point of view, I don't want anything more to do with you. So you needn't bother coming to my house hoping to get a welcome, because that won't happen,' said Karen clearly upset about her discovery.

'However I do expect you to provide maintenance money for me and William,' continued Karen who was now shaking with rage and looking around the room for something to throw. The only thing she could come up with was a chair cushion which she aimed at Spencer with some force, catching him full in the face, but not actually hurting him. After venting her anger Karen said goodbye to Glenda and stormed out of the house.

Glenda, although unhappy with the situation, took an entirely different view. Well aware that she had married Spencer before Karen, knew that her marriage was valid, but Karen's was illegal. The scam of unlawful marriage was also increased by the use of the adopted false surname of 'Evans' which was not the correct name of the groom.

Glenda, believing that she was the one and only true spouse eventually forgave Spencer for his indiscretion of bigamy towards Karen and life in the Andrews household continued more or less as it did before.

Before Spencer could leave Glenda's house he was passed a letter, the content which indicated that he was summoned to appear in court on Jury Service. This was the last thing Spencer wanted as he was having great difficulty in dividing his time up without having additional unscheduled activities to add to his diary. Also the fact that he was a serial law breaker prayed heavenly on his mind, knowing that as a Juror he could be responsible for sending criminals to prison.

The details required by the courts indicating that he was required for legal decision making covering five working days.

Chapter 9 In Court

On day one of Spencer's appearance in court as part of the Jury service, he was led into one of the bench seats along with eleven other persons, who took their seats waiting for the first case to commence.   A more reluctant juror could not ever be imagined. Spencer didn't want to be there and demonstrated his displeasure by ignoring any contact with the other jurors.

The judge appeared and took his seat. The Clerk of the Court announced that the first case on the days agenda was a man defending a bigamy case.   Out of all the crimes that existed in the world, this was the only one that he wished would not come up for his partial contribution in an arbitral decision.

The defendant was asked if he wished any members of the Jury to be replaced.   The defendant indicated that he did want to make some changes. Spencer prayed that one of those selected would be him. He even looked at the defendant menacingly hoping that an expression of terror might sway a decision to have him removed.   The defendant eventually selected two persons he wished to change, but unfortunately not one of them chosen was Spencer. Spencer's efforts to cajole through the powers of transmission of thoughts to this unfortunate person's mind had failed, so he had to make the best of the situation.

The case commenced and the defendant announced his name as Donald Featherstone and made a plea of not guilty. Spencer noticed an uncontrolled nervousness about the man. He certainly didn't look like a man that would knowingly break the law, but he was here in court at the mercy of Spencer and the other eleven Jurors.

When Featherstone took the stand his nerves were so bad that he almost collapsed and needed help from a court official to straighten up.

Featherstone did agree that he had married twice although there was some doubt about his date of divorce. The defendant claimed that he was married to his first wife who he was trying to divorce. He had received the 'decree nisi' certificate and was waiting for the 'decree absolute' arranged through his Solicitor which was due to follow six weeks and one day later.

It was proven by the prosecution that he had remarried on the day before the decree absolute was due to be released believing that he had not acted within the law, although admitted that he hadn't received the documentary evidence which provided the confirmation. The prosecution presented a calendar as well as the decree nisi certificate and decree absolute certificate.

The Jury was asked to retire to deliberate on the findings on whether he had acted within or outside of the law. Spencer was unfortunately nominated as the Jury's foreman, which was a job he was reluctant to undertake but pressured to take through the democratic vote of the others.

This was an easy case for the Jury because the defendant had undoubtedly acted outside the law as the decree absolute had not been issued portraying a date one day later than the day of Featherstone's second marriage. Spencer was most uncomfortable about the whole case and saw himself standing in the dock awaiting to be sentenced adopting the same nervous reaction as the defendant. Yet he was about to condemn an unfortunate individual who had somehow managed to get his dates wrong.

The Jury retired and in the privacy of a locked room, the case was discussed in intricate detail amongst them. Spencer adopted the view that the man had made an innocent mistake and should be released. One of the women juror's called Julie, was horrified by Spencer's stance and even doubted the decision her and the others made to make him foreman, a job Spencer did his best to avoid. Julie stood up and confronted Spencer to make her point.

'Which ever way you look at it, this man has broken the law of the land and should be severely punished for his behaviour. A person cannot get married in this country if he already has a living wife,' said Julie who put her point over quite eloquently.

The other ten Jurors were in agreement with Julie, so Spencer found himself on his own with his opinions. Although he desperately tried to press his concepts forcibly to change the views of the other eleven to save the defendant, it didn't sound convincing enough, so Spencer reluctantly was forced to change his mind to accord with the others.

The time came when the Jurors had to return to court and give their selected verdict.

The Judge turned to the Jury and addressed Spencer the foreman who, aware of his own circumstances, was not happy about the verdict he was to give.

'Members of the Jury, have you reached a verdict?' asked the Judge.

'Yes, we have your Honour,' replied Spencer.

'What have you decided,' asked the Judge.

There was a long pause as Spencer gathered his thoughts together. Thoughts of the decision made that he was unhappy to convey to the court.

'We find the defendant guilty as charged,' said Spencer. As Spencer said these words, it was like a knife going through the centre of his heart. He didn't seem interested in the punishment that was to be levied out to the poor unfortunate Featherstone that stood shame faced in the dock. His mind was totally elsewhere.

When it came to the next item before the court, which was a robbery with violence case, ironically the defendant selected Spencer to be removed from the Juror's bench and substituted for another person.

As the days passed Spencer was unable to remove the court case from his mind or the very nervous Featherstone. He along with eleven others was instrumental in sentencing a person for bigamy, at the same time realising that he had knowingly committed the exact crime albeit in far greater proportions.

At the end of his jury term he returned to his usual employment, but mused that he had witnessed a taste of what could come, should his own crime be exposed. He didn't relish the idea of being in Featherstone's position, awaiting the decision of a jury of twelve.

Chapter 10 Jim's Revenge

The next time Karen saw her brother Jim, she related to him the events that occurred in Bridges Bistro. Jim listened intently to Karen's confession that she had embarked unknowingly in a bigamist relationship with Spencer, relating in infinite detail her shock at the point of her discovery and the subsequent events that followed.

'I knew it,' said Jim in anger, 'I thought that he was already married.   Although I never went to his wedding, I can remember some of the other drivers from the depot going.   I just had that vague doubt of whether it was him getting married or one of the other drivers.   I just couldn't be certain.'

'Well I wish you had remembered at the time, it would have saved a lot of problems. The man has completely ruined my life,' said Karen.

'I never did like the man and I said at your reception that you had made a big mistake in marrying him.   I think I'll have to teach him a lesson, one that he is not likely to forget in a hurry,' continued Jim.

'Now listen here Jim, I don't want you to go to the police about this,' replied Karen.

'Why ever not?' asked Jim, 'he deserves all he gets and the sooner he is put away, the safer other women will be.'

'Although I am very angry with Spencer, I must consider William. We need to rely on Spencer's money for our upkeep. We will get nothing from him if he ends up in jail,' said Karen.

Jim was livid on hearing these revelations regarding the bogus marriage to his sister and would have derived great enjoyment from exposing Spencer to the long arm of the law. He would have considered it a just retribution for the way he had treated Karen and his own job loss to which he always regarded Spencer as the main instigator.

'Alright Karen, I will abide with your wishes for now, but Spencer is not going to get away with this, you mark my words,' assured Jim, who was pounding up and down the room in anger.

'And that's another thing. I don't want any physical violence, that's something you must promise,' urged Karen.

'Well, that is something I cannot promise,' replied Jim who stormed off out of the house in a temper.

*

In view of what had happened in Bridge's Bistro and Glenda's house when Spencer's bigamist capers were aired to the diners in a restaurant, Spencer thought it prudent not to embark on any more visits to Karen, at least for a while, whilst he was in Birmingham. However, there was his son William to consider, so contact could not be completely ruled out.

Spencer had made up his mind that the next visit he had to make was solely to see Glenda and the four children, Malcolm, Norma, Quilly and Patricia.

First he was to do some shopping. He was going through one of the market malls when Karen's brother, Jim saw him and unbeknown to Spencer promptly followed. Jim could hardly believe his good fortune when he saw Spencer making his way through crowds of people on his way out of the shopping mall. Spencer continued towards a bus stop where he stood alone waiting for the arrival of the first bus, when, without warning, he was suddenly dragged from behind by Jim with an arm around the neck in a headlock grip and dragged into a nearby alleyway.

'Got you at last,' shouted Jim as he looked around to make sure that no other person saw him.

'Now Jim, don't do anything stupid that you may regret,' said a frightened Spencer as he tried to back away.

Jim just grinned and then laughed as he grabbed hold of Spencer by the collar. Now although Spencer was tall in stature, he loathed violence and was completely unskilled in physical pugilistic contact sports and therefore was no match against the overweight Jim Walker.

'I've wanted to do this for some time,' said Jim as he laid into Spencer with a barrage of punches. Spencer did his best to parry the fists that were coming his direction with such force, but was unable to restrain Karen's brother imposing his will on him. Before Spencer could draw breath his nose was bleeding, his eye was swelling up and he had severe bruising on the chest. Still the fists were coming at him.

'Now this is one for getting me the sack,' shouted Jim as he directed a further punch to the chest.

'And this is one for marrying my sister,' continued Jim as he made another hit just below the rib cage.

'And this is one for creating bigamy with my sister,' said Jim as he landed his fist into Spencer's face.

'And this is one because I don't like you anyway,' shouted Jim as he drove another punch into the side of Spencer's head.

'And this is one for good measure, just in case there is anything I've forgotten,' yelled Jim.

'I'll call the police for this assault,' said Spencer who found it difficult to speak because of the pain.

'No you won't, because you are a bigamist, and bigamy is against the law. You, my friend will not be telling anyone about this,' confirmed Jim with a wry smile, 'also I would advise you not to show your face around here again.'

On that comment Jim left the scene of the assault, leaving Spencer writhing in agony curled up in a foetal position on the ground with his arms clutching his chest.

Spencer tried to get up but the pain in his chest was too bad to make further movement. A man walking down the alleyway stopped with shock at seeing a person lying on the ground bleeding and ran over to Spencer to help him on his feet.

'Are you alright,' said the stranger as he tried to help him to his feet.

'Yes, nothing that a few days in rehab won't cure,' replied Spencer as he struggled to remain in the standing position but still needed the assistance of the stranger.

'Have you been mugged? Did he steal anything? Do you think we ought to call for an ambulance? Do you think we ought to call the police?' said the stranger who bombarded Spencer with lots of questions but seemed very willing to help.

'No! I haven't been mugged. No! Nothing has been stolen. No! I don't think it is necessary to call an ambulance or involve the police. However I would be grateful if you could help me onto a bus,' requested Spencer. The helpful stranger did as requested.

On the bus, Spencer started to think about the blackmailing tactics that Jim had adopted by telling him to stay away and realised that he could be bullied at any time by Jim. He pondered that whatever punishment Jim levied out to him, there was nothing that he could do about it.

Spencer decided that he could not see Glenda and the four children while at Birmingham in this visit, being the injured state that he was. This would only promote too many awkward questions, which Spencer would have difficulty in answering. Instead he got off the bus inched his way to his lorry, clambered in the cab and rested while he retrieved his breath and nursed his wounds.

Chapter 11　A Visit to Portsmouth

Spencer's Diary indicated Janet, who was heavily pregnant, was due a visit in Portsmouth. However a visit to see Janet was always combined with a visit to call on Holly who also lived in the same town. A quick look at his notes, which he kept in the front locker of his cab, reminded him that he had a daughter called Olga and two boys called Richard and Stanley at Holly's home. Also at Janet's home there was just the single child called Vera. With so many wives and children, Spencer would practice remembering these names prior to making a visit.

Spencer made the decision to call on Holly first with a view to staying over night. The next day he offered to take the family to the local park, where he would indulge in a kick about with a football to amuse the boys.

Richard who was six years old liked to show off his soccer ability by kicking the ball as hard as he could. On one occasion he demonstrated how hard he could kick by booting the ball a distance of one hundred and fifty feet into a crowd of people. Spencer wasn't sure if the ball hit anyone and asked Richard to retrieve it.

'Now quickly, go and get the ball and don't forget to say sorry,' explained Spencer.

Richard ran off eager to please his father by bringing back the ball, but when he reached the crowd of people a woman had picked the ball up, looking around for the person who kicked it.

Spencer began to follow Richard believing that as a parent he should also apologise, but stopped in his steps when he saw the woman who held the ball. It happened to be Janet and his daughter Vera was with her. Had she seen him? Maybe she had been concentrating on the little boy running towards her. She didn't call out to Spencer, so he thought that maybe he hadn't been seen.

Spencer turned round and retraced his steps towards Holly who was enjoying watching all the action. Noticing Janet made him aware that he had to remove himself from the park as quickly as possible. Seeing two wives within the range of two hundred feet of each other was too much for Spencer to endure any possible embarrassment. He had to make a rapid excuse to Holly to leave the park.

'Look Holly, I have just remembered, there is a man I arranged to meet to go over some business,' said an agitated Spencer anxious to make himself scarce.

'What, are you leaving us,' replied Holly.

'Yes, I'll only be half an hour and when I return I'll meet you at the duck pond,' replied Spencer.

After making his apologies to Holly he discretely left the Park at the same time making sure he didn't bump into Janet and Vera.

In the meantime Janet followed Richard, who was carrying the ball, and heading towards his mother.

'Oh, I just wanted to make sure this little boy was alright and wasn't on his own,' Janet said to Holly as she approached.

'No it's okay, he's with me,' replied Holly. The two women started to strike up a conversation and appeared to be enjoying each other's company. They talked about the children, their husbands and their own home lives. They soon came to realise that they had quite a lot in common, particularly in regard to their husbands.

'Won't you join us? I'm just waiting for my husband to turn up. He shouldn't be too long, I'll introduce him to you,' suggested Holly.

'Okay, although I can only stay for a short time, because I'm expecting my husband to call at any time and I don't want to miss him,' replied Janet.

'What do you mean by call on you?' enquired Holly.

'Well, I don't see a lot of him. You see, he is a long distance lorry driver,' replied Janet.

'I know exactly what you mean, my husband is in the same type of work,' replied Holly.

The two women continued chatting away and seemed to be getting on famously. Then Spencer returned back to the park and started to make his way to the duck pond as he had previously arranged with Holly.

To his utter surprise he could see the two women talking and quickly turned about and retraced his steps to the park exit. After a further hour he returned to discover that Janet had left and therefore he felt that he had been given the all clear to safely rejoin Holly and the three children.

'I thought you would only be half an hour seeing your friend,' challenged Holly.

'Sorry babe,' my talks with him went on longer than I thought,' said Spencer.

To Spencer's surprise Holly did not appear to be too upset by his lateness, her mind seemed to be on other matters.

'Do you know, I met this lovely woman by the name of Janet who has a little girl called Vera,' informed Holly.

'That's nice,' said Spencer, shocked that they had been getting on so well.

'Yes, and best of all she lives around here,' replied an excited Holly.

'You know you shouldn't get involved with strangers,' said Spencer.

'Well, we are strangers no longer, because we have arranged to meet up,' informed Holly.

'Oh, that's not a very good idea, you don't know anything about her,' replied Spencer who was desperately trying to alter Holly's plans at the same time fearing the worst.

'I must tell you this,' said Holly, 'Janet has a husband by the same name as you, and it gets even better because he also is a lorry driver. The name 'Spencer' is such a rare name. Don't you find that a tremendous coincidence?'

Spencer was getting really agitated, uncomfortably moving his head from side to side trying to think of a suitable reply.

'You're right, my name is unusual which makes the coincidence even more remarkable,' said Spencer after a long pause.

The family all went home to Holly's house. As soon as they went through the front door, Spencer went into every room in the house looking for any photographs that Holly may have displayed on the walls showing him in them. He needed to do this because he remembered that this was how Karen caught him out when she discovered an incriminating snapshot in Glenda's house. Fortunately there were none, so Spencer was able to compose himself and heave a sigh of relief.

The next thing Spencer had to do was to see Janet as soon as possible to ensure that her house was not marred by photographs on open display that showed him in them. Janet's house was different, because it was discovered that she had two on display in the lounge.

'Those two photographs you have on the walls,' said Spencer.

'What about them?' asked Janet.

'I don't like them much. Can I take them down?'

'Why don't you like them?' asked Janet.

'Because they are not very good photo's of either of us,' replied Spencer.

'Alright, remove them if you must,' said Janet.

Spencer didn't require telling twice, he took the two photographs off the wall, removed them from their frames and tore them up into very small pieces, much to the surprise of Janet.

'Do you know, I met a lovely women in the park today called Holly,' said Janet.

Spencer sat in a chair waiting for the next thing she was going to say which he predicted almost word for word.

'You wouldn't believe it but this women I met has a husband with the same Christian name as you and even more incredible does the same kind of work,' said Janet.

'Oh, is that right,' replied Spencer who was getting rather bored with the conversation which seemed to be very similar to the one he had with Holly.

'You don't seem to agree on how incredible that is. In fact you appear to be most disinterested by what I am telling you,' said Janet.

'I just think it is a dangerous thing to do,' replied Spencer.

'What is?' queried Janet.

'Talking to people you don't even know,' replied Spencer who was eager to prevent a friendship developing between the two women.

'Now you listen to me Spencer. I talk to who I like. I make my own friends and furthermore I don't want any interference from you,' replied Janet who was clearly angry at the way the conversation was going and Spencer dictating to her.

Spencer tried his best to placate his partner and by the end of the evening he had succeeded in calming her down. The evening finished up with the two of them and Vera going out to dinner in a local restaurant. The following day Spencer was back on the road.

The friendship between Holly and Janet continued to develop and eventually they would alternate between their addresses for tea, cakes and cosy chats. They would sometimes discuss their husbands, not realising that their spouses were the same person. Spencer became extremely uncomfortable by the friendship of his two wives, believing that it was only a matter of time before the whole secrecy of his bigamist activities would come out into the open. Any exposure would be sufficiently spicy to circulate by gossip through Portsmouth and was eventually bound to attract universal media attention in the National Newspapers.

There was of course the added problem that any visits to Holly could be dangerous if Janet happened to be there when he called. The situation was exactly the same if he visited Janet's house and Holly suddenly appeared. Also similar to the Glenda and Karen scenario, the two woman attempted to arrange foursome nights out, which included the two husbands. Spencer was beginning to realise how ridiculous he had been in his choice of woman in the same Town. He mused, that however unlikely they were to meet up in a large town, there was always a remote chance that they could.

In reality Spencer needed twice the amount of hours in a day, enough time to do his work and sufficient time to keep pace with his well organised diary. It became a mammoth task to make the various phone calls to all his partners and make carefully scheduled arrangements, at the same time mindful that when he did arrive at an address, there would be no surprises to greet him.

Chapter 12   A Problem with Iris

Eight months after hearing the news from Janet about her pregnancy, twins Xavia and Yvonne were born.   Although his third wife Iris was never likely to meet these little girls, she was nevertheless destined to pay for their upbringing together with the rest of Spencer's brood.   This was an unscheduled expense which Iris was completely unaware and would surely be devastated if she knew the truth.

It was one day in May that Spencer received a call from Iris on his mobile phone.   The call appeared urgent, because Iris requested that Spencer call into the Manor at Torbay immediately to see her.

Spencer realising that something serious may have occurred, treated the request as something that required rapid attention and headed off to Devonshire immediately.

On arrival Iris seemed very upset.   Her eyes were red from crying and she appeared to have lost a lot of weight.

'We have got to move from here and buy something smaller,' said Iris, 'I've just heard from my bank and I have hardly anything left in it,' said Iris.

'Why, what has happened? Where has it all gone?' asked Spencer.

'The upkeep of this large house has drained all my savings. Also you haven't helped. You have been taking out large amounts of money for your own purposes. The curious thing is that I don't see anything tangible for the money you have withdrawn,' said Iris turning the financial problem on Spencer.

'Why, would you like me to give you a breakdown of my expenditure?' said Spencer angrily believing that attacking Iris was the best form of defence.

Iris was taken aback by Spencer's sudden mood swing of aggressiveness and tried to soften the situation.

'No, that won't be necessary, just go careful in future,' replied Iris.

Spencer sighed with relief that his bluff had worked. He would have to be an expert accountant and accomplished magician all rolled into one, if Iris pressed him for details of his expenditure. However, Spencer had a greater problem. What was he going to do about the instant drop in his allowances, which he so generously distributed amongst his five wives. He was aware that Iris could no longer be relied upon for a source of income, so he had to look elsewhere. Whatever had to be done, had to be resolved and executed quickly. He also realised that due to Iris's drop in wealth, she would have turned from a provider into a financial liability, which would mean that Iris would be looking to him for monetary support. Spencer knew that somehow he had to make some quick changes to his lifestyle.

The answer had to be to find another wife, although this time she had to be a person with money. Although Spencer vowed to himself that he would never take another wife he was aware that needs must. For Spencer, this was not going to be easy, as he was unlikely to find anyone of wealth in the cafes and pubs that he frequented. He thought long and hard about this problem, considering the few options he placed at his disposal for meeting someone of wealth. Finally he decided that the answer was to take a holiday. Not just any holiday. It had to be a cruise. Not just any cruise. The criteria had to be an expensive cruise, possibly one to cover travelling around half of the globe. The theory being, *'the more expensive the cruise, the wealthier the passengers travelling on it.'* Spencer opined that there were a lot of rich widows who were on their own on cruises, who would like the opportunity of meeting someone for some romantic liaisons.

It was decided, Spencer would borrow the money from the bank, which he regarded as a speculative investment and go on a 'no expense spared' cruise.

*

Spencer queued to go on the ship which was waiting in Southampton Dock. His eyes consistently working overtime as he carefully looked and considered every female passenger in the line up, making a mental note of those standing on their own. He was definitely on a mission and one that had to succeed. His selection did not need to be a woman of good appearance or young, but what she did need was wealth, the main criteria of his mission. She also needed to be keen to marry him, because after all, not only did she need to support all his families, Spencer also needed to be recompensed for the speculative cost of the cruise and the recovery of his lost wages.

On the ship, Spencer wasted no time in talking to as many of the female passengers as he could find. He regarded the cruise, not as a vacation of pleasure, but a time to put his well practised 'pulling' skills to the test. The ship offered much entertainment and many pleasures of interest, such as shows, quizzes, dance classes, etcetera, however Spencer was not interested in any of these activities, because they limited any chance of conversational communication. So he restricted his choices to excursions, daytime ship bars and dances in the evening. He also mused that it was unlikely he was going to get any single women on his dining table in the restaurant, so this also was likely to be ruled out for meeting anyone.

Spencer worked really hard, adopting the use of his silver tongue at the bar and dancing the night away with as many single women as he could, plying with drinks those he had selected for the possible advancement of his quest. His speculative efforts were costing him dearly, but to Spencer's dismay he didn't seem to be making any headway. This was because the single wealthy women were categorised in three types, those whose husbands have recently died, those who have never married and those whose husbands had died or left them some time ago.

Spencer considered that in reality there was only one category he could target and that was the women who had been without a husband for some time. This therefore restricted him to a small minority of the female passengers.

It was the last day of the cruise and Spencer had up to then, not succeeded with his talents or with his intent. However he had six hours left and he was not ready to give up so easily. There was one woman of sixty seven years of age called Linda who had grey hair, overweight, short in stature with a double chin. Now although this women was old enough to be Spencer's mother and definitely not his normal selection for a partner, the cosy chats he had with Linda revealed that she owned a mansion in Woking Surrey, in which she employed a chef and servants to run the overall domestic duties. She also owned a villa in Spain. This was sufficient to wet Spencer's appetite and made Linda a prime target for selection. He then applied all his skills of charm and patter to impress Linda and in so doing considered that he had made the last day of his cruise well worthwhile.

Linda was jolly and had a tremendous personality, loved dancing and fine wines and Spencer ensured that in the short time he had left remaining on the ship that he would never leave her side. He also wasted no time in obtaining her telephone number and arranging to meet up after they left the ship.

Spencer still had a lot of work to do on Linda after his holiday. He would meet up with her on a regular basis, affording her absolute priority in the time that he was with her, over his other five wives. When he felt the time was right Spencer made his well rehearsed proposal of marriage to her.

'I would love to marry you,' said Linda, 'but how do I know that you only want marriage to get at my money?'

'You can't be sure about anything in life, but I have to say that I am truly hurt by your comment. If you really believe that is my sole intention, then you must say 'No' straight away,' said Spencer looking forlorn. In saying this it was an all or nothing gamble. He then thought it was necessary to assist Linda in her decision making by doing a bit of play acting. He commenced by turning his back on Linda and started to walk away. His steps were short and slow with the purpose of giving Linda plenty of time to call him back.

After ten paces with his head hanging down Spencer wondered whether he had failed in the gamble of Linda's affections, then after a further step Spencer heard the call he was longing for.

'Not so fast,' said Linda, 'come back, of course we will get married. We will do it as soon as possible.'

Spencer turned around and retraced his steps back towards Linda and gave her a big hug and a kiss. He was ecstatic that Linda had accepted his proposal. His speculative venture of cruising to find a wealthy partner had eventually paid off. No longer did he have to worry about money for his families, who were always after him to improve their financial stability.

'So when do you want to embark on this special union?' asked Linda.

'Leave it to me, I will make all the necessary arrangements,' replied Spencer.

Now in the past, marriages to his other partners were not complimented with the offer of Spencer's help. However in this case he wanted to do it all. The first job was to book the Registry Office at the earliest possible date. This was to ensure Linda's window of opportunity for changing her mind was minimised. Also the earlier he could set a wedding date, the sooner he could access her money.

*

Spencer intended this to be his final marriage. One thing in his favour was that his bride was too elderly to have children, so he regarded this purely as a marriage of convenience. He never had any romantic tendencies towards Linda and hoped that during the course of the marriage that she would not pursue him too much to make the union one where sex was a prime factor.

The wedding, as expected was a lavish affair with the appearance of no expense being spared. The alcohol flowed as if there was an exhaustible supply just waiting to be drunk. The numerous guests took full advantage of the good food and hospitality afforded by Linda.

Spencer was always asked the question by the new bride regarding the lack of guests invited by the groom. He was used to this question, having been asked it many times before, so he was well equipped with his usual stock answer, which seemed to be accepted by those who expressed an interest into his solitary life.

When the wedding was over and home life started to take a more settled format, Spencer approached his new bride about paying for the cruise which had left him in considerable debt with the bank.

'Linda, I must inform you that I do not have very much money and barely sufficient to live on adequately and hope that you are in a position to help me out,' said Spencer, who although is usually prone to telling lies, was on this occasion actually telling the truth.

'How much do you need?' asked Linda.

'Oh, I think twenty thousand pounds will cover it,' said Spencer hardly changing his expression when mentioning the large amount.

'That's a lot of money,' gasped Linda.

'Well, I did owe a lot of money on the cruise where I met you, which has put me in a debit situation with the bank, and I know that you would not want me to be in debt,' explained Spencer.

Linda said no more but immediately found her cheque book and wrote Spencer out a payment for the requested amount without any further comment. The ease by which he was able to achieve his requirement gave him confidence that any future monetary instability, could be easily solved by appealing to Linda's generosity.

Spencer was amazed at the huge residence that Linda owned, which had ten bedrooms with ensuite bathrooms, huge sitting rooms and a medium sized indoor swimming pool. This form of opulence was luxury in the extreme, something of which Spencer was totally unaccustomed. It even excelled beyond the ostentatious qualities of the Mansion owned by Iris.

'All this finery will take me some time to get used to,' he said to Linda.

'Well enjoy it, because everything here is now shared between us,' replied Linda as she put her arms around him.

'Amazing, this is like a big win on the lottery,' said Spencer as his eyes tried to take in everything around him.

'Now listen Spencer, you don't have to work anymore, so give up that job of yours and stay here with me,' insisted Linda.

'No I can't do that. I like to think that I am helping in some way and in order to assist in providing for my keep, I will have to keep on working. The only problem is that I will not be home every night because my work takes me abroad to make deliveries, so I hope you don't mind,' said a convincing Spencer.

'No of course not, if you feel that is what you have to do. In fact I admire your resolve,' replied an understanding Linda.

Spencer delighted that Linda was so understanding, by not placing any restrictions on him, meant that there would be no deviation from his other lifestyle of making visits to his remaining wives and children. He had successfully achieved his quest of securing additional finance for his ever increasing family. This eased the problems facing him on maintenance, the only difference being that Linda was the main benefactor instead of Iris who due to a sudden decline in wealth, could no longer be relied upon for any support.

Spencer felt that the marriage to Linda was the best thing he had ever done. Not only did it give him financial security, it provided him with a very dear companion who doted over him and spoilt him rotten, to the extent that he could do no wrong.

Spencer added Linda's name to the list he kept in his cab, which was getting longer and longer every time there was a wedding or a new child was born. He believed when adding Linda's name that it would be the last addition to his list which looked as follows:

My Family

Wife's Name	Children Boys	Children Girls	Location
Glenda Andrews	Malcolm Quilly	Norma Patricia	Birmingham
Holly Butcher	Richard Stanley	Olga	Portsmouth
Iris Chandler	Thomas	Ursula	Torbay
Janet Drake		Vera Xavia Yvonne	Portsmouth
Karen Evans	William		Birmingham
Linda Fitzgerald	(No Children)		Woking

The union to Linda had continued two years when Spencer received a disturbing telephone call from one of the household servants. Apparently Linda had been taken to hospital complaining about pains in her upper chest. When the news was received, it was sufficiently bad for Spencer to turn his lorry in a different direction to make an unscheduled call at the hospital. When he arrived he was informed that Linda was in a coma, had breast cancer which had travelled to other parts of her body and was therefore not expected to live long.

Spencer stayed by her side, holding her hand, talking to her all the time, even though she was unable to respond. During the night the end finally came to Linda who never did come out of her coma.

It came as a terrible blow to Spencer, because amongst all the wives that he had, he adored Linda the most. She was the one person who never asked him for anything or expected anything from him. Spencer was allowed to do exactly what he wanted without any query from Linda and she spoilt him terribly. He was genuinely distraught at her sudden death and inconsolable during the time leading up to her funeral, which he had dutifully arranged.

Although he kept the servants on at the mansion, Spencer was too upset to spend any time there. The constant reminder of Linda not being there, kept him away. He was however contacted by solicitors about the content of the will. It appeared that Linda had left everything to him both in money and tangible assets.

It wasn't long before Spencer was approached by Linda's son and daughter regarding the unfairness of their mother's decision, who threatened to make an appeal through the legal system. Spencer however, appreciated that it would be inequitable to regard himself as the sole beneficiary and agreed with Linda's children that he would only take twenty five percent of the total assets awarded to him, leaving the remainder to be divided equally between them. This solution, after the payments to Linda's son and daughter left Spencer still a very rich man.

Chapter 13 William

Spencer was driving towards Reading when he received a telephone call from Karen on his mobile phone. This was unusual because after the discovery that he had another wife in Glenda she had become completely estranged. She tried to keep Spencer away from the house and always did her best not to contact him.

The substance of the telephone call was in regard to twelve year old William. His school headmaster had specifically requested to see Spencer. Karen said that he didn't give a date or time, but asked that Spencer call into the school to see him.

Spencer thought that the call might be important enough to make the effort to see him urgently that day. After dropping his load of children's toys at a Reading store he headed off to Birmingham where he met the headmaster. The staff head was a Mr Compton, short in stature with a thick greying hair. He had a stern manner about him and announced on meeting him that he hadn't a lot of time to spare.

'Thank you for calling in to see me Mr. Evans, we seem to be having a few problems at the school with young William,' said Compton.

'Oh dear. What has he been up to?' asked Spencer who was not used to being called Evans, the name he chose when he married Karen.

'Truancy, bad school report, bad behaviour in the classroom and generally out of control,' replied Compton.

'That doesn't sound good at all, I shall have a word with him,' said Spencer.

'I think it is going to need more than a word. It needs stricter parenting, disciplinary actions, ensuring he does his homework and a parent walking him to school every day so that he is not tempted to play truancy,' insisted Compton.

'Have you spoken to him recently Mr Compton?' asked Spencer.

'Yes I have, and there seems to be a lack of fatherly parenting in the Evans household. He complains that he hardly ever sees you,' replied Compton.

'That is probably true. You see William's mother and I are estranged. I won't enlarge on the reasons why. Suffice to say that I hardly see anything of William or his mother in the course of a month and when I do make the rare visit, I am not allowed to stay for any length of time,' said Spencer.

'Well that's not ideal for a young lad growing up. No wonder he is the way he is,' replied Compton.

'What are his general learning skills like?' asked Spencer.

'Very poor. I put him to the test on his spelling. I asked him to spell 'onomatopoeia'. Do you know he didn't even know where to start,' replied Compton.

'I'm not sure that I would know how to spell that, so I'm sure a twelve year old wouldn't have a clue. What does the word mean?' enquired Spencer.

'It means a word that imitates the sound it represents like for example 'moo' the sound that a cow makes or 'hiss' the steam that escapes from a fractured pipe. I thought everyone knew that,' said Compton disgusted that Spencer would not know the meaning of this simple word.

'Everyone except me,' replied Spencer, 'I would suggest if you are going to test a twelve year old by asking him to spell a word, then you would choose something a little simpler.'

'I am the head of this school and my methods of teaching should not be open to question,' replied Compton annoyed that Spencer had tried to give him advice.

'Is he in school today?' asked Spencer.

'No! As a matter of fact he isn't,' replied Compton.

'Would you think it would help if I had a word with his mother, as you don't appear to see an awful lot of your son?' asked Compton.

'No. I will speak with Karen on the subject. Thank you Mr. Compton for your help,' replied Spencer.

'One last message I have for you Mr. Evans. If his behaviour doesn't improve within the next four weeks, then I will have no alternative than to expel him,' warned Compton.

Spencer went straight back to Karen regarding the discussions he had had at the school, the words of Compton wringing in his ears.

As Spencer was not allowed to just walk into the house anymore, he knocked on the door. When Karen saw Spencer standing on the door step, she promptly tried to close it. Spencer put his foot in the door to prevent full closure.

'Listen Karen I have come to speak to you about William. I have just seen his headmaster,' remonstrated Spencer.

'Well, I suppose you'd better come in and tell me about it,' said Karen begrudgingly.

Once inside the house, Spencer looked around and noticed that since he was last there, Karen had made many changes in the house, reminding him that it had been some time since he was last there.

'What did the headmaster have to say that was so important?' asked Karen.

'He said that William was totally out of control and regularly missed school,' reported Spencer.

'It's the first I've heard of it,' replied Karen.

'Where is he today?' asked Spencer.

'At school,' answered Karen.

'That's the point Mr. Compton the headmaster was making. He is not there today,' replied Spencer.

'Well he should be, he left for school this morning,' insisted Karen.

'Listen Karen you have to allow me more access to William,' said Spencer.

Karen pulled a face as if to demonstrate that she didn't agree.

'Why should I allow you back into this house over what you have done to me?' replied Karen.

'Because if you don't, William will be expelled from school,' replied Spencer.

Spencer realised that due to past events and the secret that they both shared, he was in no position to insist on anything. He was totally at Karen's mercy.

'Alright then, but it is on condition that you do not come into this house. You can have access to take him out on either a Saturday or a Sunday,' insisted Karen.

Spencer was in no position to argue and realised that this was the best offer he was going to get. Spencer was about to leave the house, when William walked in. He walked over to his father and gave him a hug.

'Where have you been?' asked Karen who was still angered by what she had recently heard.

'I've been at school,' replied William.

'Don't lie, according to Mr. Compton you haven't been there all day,' said Karen as she cuffed the boy around the ear.

'Don't hit him,' protested Spencer.

'Well then, you're his father, you sort him out,' insisted Karen as she left to walk into the kitchen.

'Listen William, I've just seen your headmaster and he hasn't given me a good report of you. You have to change and you have to change from today. What do you want to do when you grow up?' asked Spencer.

'I want to be an Architect,' replied William without hesitation.

'Well then, to become an Architect you have to put in a lot of study hours, which means doing your homework and not bunking off school,' explained Spencer.

'Okay,' replied William.

'Now William, promise me that you will try to do your very best at school and also help your mother,' whispered Spencer.

'I promise,' said William as he shamefully hung his head.

'Now I will be calling in more often and I will ask your mum, about your schooling and if you have helped her at home. Oh, and one more thing. It is wrong to tell lies,' said Spencer.

'Karen, can you start to walk with him to school again? It is a request that the headmaster has made and I said I would ask you about it,' said Spencer.

'Alright then, but I do expect you to do your bit,' insisted Karen.

'Before I leave, can you spell 'onomatopoeia?' asked Spencer.

'That's an odd request, but I'll do it,' said Karen.

Karen spelt it perfectly without pausing to think between the letters.

'Do you know what it means?' asked Spencer.

'Of course I do. It's a word which copies the sound it's meant to represent like 'dong' the sound a bell makes,' said Karen, 'I thought everyone would know that.'

'Well, I must confess I didn't know it,' said Spencer.

'Why do you ask?' asked Karen.

'Oh, Compton put the question to me and I didn't know the answer,' said Spencer.

'You must have felt very silly, not knowing a simple thing like that,' remarked Karen.

'Well in a way I suppose I did, I did feel a bit foolish,' replied Spencer.

Spencer left Karen's house happier than he was when he first arrived but also feeling rather stupid that he didn't know some of the more important words in the English language.

Chapter 14 Jobs for the Children

The years rolled by so did the ages of Glenda's children who were 20 years of age for twins Malcolm and Norma, also eighteen years of age for Quilly and Patricia. It was time for Spencer to visit Glenda's household to celebrate the birthdays of the two eldest children.

The two young men and two young women were always pleased to see Spencer which always received a big hug whenever they greeted each other.

'Well tell your father the good news,' prompted Glenda with a bit of a nudge into Malcolm's back.

'Yes, I have just secured a job Dad,' said Malcolm with glee.

'Oh, and what are you doing in employment?' enquired Spencer, delighted that his son was working for a living.

'I'm working in the Police Force,' replied Malcolm beaming all over his face.

Spencer who was secretly shocked by his son's revelation of employment, tried to hide his discomfort with an enigmatic smile. Anything to do with the police made him nervous and uncomfortable.

'Oh that's nice, well done,' replied Spencer.

'That's not all, Norma also has a job which she managed to secure since you were here last,' said Glenda.

'Come on Norma, don't keep me in suspense,' said Spencer eager to hear what she had to impart.

'My job is not nearly as interesting as Malcolm's. I work for the Council,' said Norma.

'Oh, that's good. Doing what?' asked Spencer.

'I'm working in the Registrar's Office, registering births, deaths and marriages,' said Norma.

Spencer was drinking a cup of tea at the time, then choked, coughed and splattered at hearing Norma's reply.

'Sorry about that, I think my tea went down the wrong way,' said Spencer.

'It doesn't finish there,' said Glenda, 'because Malcolm has also managed to get Quilly in the

Police force. Also Patricia has just secured herself a job last week.'

'Don't tell me, let me guess,' said Spencer, 'working in a Solicitor's office.'

'How did you know that?' asked Patricia, mystified that her father guessed so accurately and correctly without clue or prompt.

'Oh, it figures. It couldn't really be anything else,' said Spencer.

Patricia remained looking puzzled. Spencer in the meantime was thinking that there were forces conspiring against him that would destine his four children to take jobs all associate with the law or businesses that could easily expose his criminal activities.

'How are you getting on Norma. Do you find your job interesting?' asked Spencer.

'I find it extremely interesting. Do you know, we managed to discover in our records a man who had committed bigamy with not just one but two other women. Bigamy is something that is very rare in this country so when someone is caught, the legal system tend to take a strong line,' replied Norma.

'Oh dear, and what did you do about it? asked Spencer.

'Well we had no option other than to inform the police,' said Norma.

'Quite right. After all it is a crime,' said Spencer.

'Yes, and it is a crime that has to be punished. In this case it was easy, because all I had to do was tell Malcolm and he ensured it went through the proper channels to its ultimate conclusion. In this case the man was jailed,' continued Norma.

Spencer shuddered at the thought of hearing the word 'punishment' given by Norma.

'Well, I am pleased with you all, that you have managed to secure employment, although I must confess they would probably not have been the jobs I would choose,' said Spencer.

'Listen, we can't all be lorry drivers,' said Patricia.

'Yes I agree, but as you have all taken jobs associated with the legal system, always remember when you restrain a person who has broken the law, things are sometimes not always what they seem and you must never be too quick to judge a person,' pointed out Spencer.

'That's very deep Dad, I've never heard you come out with stuff like that before,' remarked Malcolm.

'No I dare say you haven't. Just remember what I have said, it might serve you in good stead during the fullness of time in your employment,' confirmed Spencer.

'I'm not sure I understand what you are trying to convey to us?' enquired a puzzled Malcolm.

'I'll give you an example. Norma has just told us, that staff going through the records in her office had come across a bigamist who had married three times over. Now although the man may have broken the law, his character as a person may be flawless. He may even have had to push himself into marriages that he didn't even want, but was forced to go ahead with it because having managed to get a girl pregnant, it was expected of him that he should do the honourable thing and marry the girl,' related Spencer.

'That's all very interesting Dad, but which ever way you look at it, he has broken the law in this country and as a result should suffer the full consequences,' replied Malcolm. 'In fact I remember you telling us that you were on Jury service and a very similar case cropped up and you and your Juror friends had no hesitation in subjecting the defendant to penal reform,' added Malcolm.

'Yes, that's perfectly true Malcolm, although we had to look at all aspects of the case before making our final decision. It's also true to say that some of the jury wanted the man released,' related Spencer.

'So what were your initial thoughts Dad before you finally committed the defendant to a guilty verdict. Were you one of those who wanted the defendant to be released?' asked Malcolm.

'I would prefer to keep quiet on what was discussed in the Juror's room, it is after all confidential stuff,' replied Spencer.

In making his observations to his four children, Spencer was obviously preparing himself for when the truth would come out. However, he was not prepared for the answer or question he received from Malcolm. He was also aware that in the professions and jobs they had taken, the awful truth about him could surface at any time. It was hoped that if it did, that it wouldn't be one of his children that had discovered it.

The twin's birthday celebrations continued late into the evening. Spencer stayed the night and was up early the next day ready to go to work.

Malcolm was also up early dressed in his police uniform. The very sight of him dressed in the dark blue gave Spencer an uncomfortable feeling inside and he began thinking that his time for others discovering his history was not too far away.

Chapter 15 The Surprise

Spencer's return to the office was always on a Wednesday. This particular Wednesday was not unusual from any other. Spencer parked up his lorry in the yard and walked towards Jerry's office. Spencer would then pick up his wages together with the schedule of the following weeks work. On his way walking towards the building a man suddenly stepped in front of him and grabbed his arm. Spencer jumped back with surprise only to find that it was Karen's brother Jim.

'What are you doing here? Has Jerry taken you back on again?' asked Spencer.

'No he hasn't, but I do need to speak with you privately. Also I would prefer that we went elsewhere for a chat as I don't want Jerry to see me here,' replied Jim.

Jim seemed calm and even a bit on the friendly side, so Spencer agreed to talk to him in the nearby cafe. Jim made sure that they found a table far from earshot of other patrons in the cafe and the two sat opposite each other.

'Now Jim what is so important that you would have to see me at work?' asked Spencer.

'Well Spencer you are a hard man to find, but I knew you would be here on a Wednesday morning,' replied Jim.

'You still haven't told me why you want to speak to me,' insisted Spencer.

'The problem is that now I haven't got a job, and as a result I have no money,' replied Jim.

'How does that affect me?' asked Spencer.

'Because you were the one that lost me my job,' replied Jim.

'I don't agree with you on that. Oh, I get it, you want me to have a word with Jerry to ask him to take you back,' replied Spencer.

'No. Not exactly. I want you to give me an allowance that I can live on,' said Jim who was quite forceful in his approach.

'You've got a cheek,' said Spencer shocked that Jim should make such a suggestion, 'first you physically take me to task and then you ask me for a regular allowance because you've lost your job.   Well the answer is a definite no.'

Spencer rose out of his chair as if to leave the cafe, even before he had ordered himself a drink.

'Sit down,' insisted Jim forcefully, 'I think you will want to hear what I have got to say.'

Spencer slowly retained his seat.

'If you don't agree to my demands, I shall go to the police regarding your bigamist activities,' insisted Jim in hushed tones just about audible so that only Spencer could hear.

'Look Jim, I have families to keep.   I can't afford to give you any money.   This is extortion by blackmail,' replied Spencer.

'Then you leave me with no alternative,' said Jim who made a move to leave his chair.

'Hold on,' urged Spencer who had grabbed hold of Jim's wrist, 'I don't know what your demands are,' said Spencer.

'Well, how does one hundred pounds sterling a week sound?' asked Jim.

'Not good and totally out of the question and I hope you are aware that blackmail is a criminal offence,' replied Spencer.

'So is bigamy. So if it is totally out of the question, then I know what I must do,' insisted Jim.

Spencer realising he would find it difficult to manage financially if he acceded to Jims demands turning Jim away to carry out his threat, he could lose everything.

'Okay Jim, I'll do it. However, I don't know how you can sleep at nights knowing what you have just done,' said Spencer.

'Oh, I'll be able to sleep better knowing that I'll have some money coming in. You never know in time, I might even get to like you,' said Jim with a smile.

Spencer grimaced at Jim's last remark and his apparent delight. He wished he could do or say something to wipe the smile from his face.

The two of them rose out of their chairs and Jim offered his hand to Spencer for a handshake which Spencer declined by placing his right hand behind his back. Both of them left the cafe. Jim, displaying a smile on his face and Spencer looking thoroughly dejected.

As Jim drove away in his car, Spencer was left to contemplate how he was going to comply with the terms that he had agreed to.

Spencer wondered if it was worth informing Karen of her brother's blackmailing proposals. However, Spencer was not exactly Karen's best fan and after consideration thought it better to remain silent about his meeting with Jim, which meant full compliance of his terms.

*

Spencer continued to pay Jim his blackmailing money, but then started to fall heavily into debt with the bank. The money he received from Linda's will had long eroded and he was left trying to juggle his money so that none of the wives were left wanting. In desperation he sought the services of a Loan Company, who were happy to lend him money without character references or the usual checks on his ability to pay. It was not long before he realised that the money lent to him together with the associated interest charges only added to his financial problems. He was therefore becoming deeper and deeper in debt resulting in him increasing the loan. As loan introduced loan and perpetuated into full scale borrowing, Spencer was at his wits end not knowing how to overcome the problem of his ever increasing debt.

In the past, the situation was resolved by finding a rich widow and marrying her. However he decided that he would no longer continue the ways of his errant past. New wives were strictly off the menu. Also he was conscious that his advancing years were not having a good effect on his appearance, so he would no longer find it quite so easy to charm a woman, the way he had done in his younger days. The only answer was to do more overtime, and clear the debt that way.

Chapter 16 Janet

Spencer consulted his diary and noticed that he was due a visit in Portsmouth, first to meet Janet and stay the night, followed by calling in on Holly. He had one visit to make at Southampton docks which was not too far from Portsmouth and then the rest of the day he intended to reserve for Janet.

Spencer's lifestyle was so intense in trying to juggle his time around his wives and his work, that it could only operate smoothly with the aid of a well documented time schedule. Everything appeared to be going like clockwork. Spencer entered Janet's house, the two embraced and then Janet then proceeded to tell Spencer all the news.

It was noticeable by Spencer that Janet's chatter was mainly about her friend Holly and from what Janet was saying Spencer got the distinct impression that they were seeing a lot of one another.

The following day, Spencer was out of bed by eight o'clock, had his breakfast and leaving the house by ten o'clock.   He said his farewells to Janet at the door and headed down the front footpath.   However to his utter surprise and dismay, he was met with Holly approaching Janet's front door.

'Hello Spencer. What are you doing here?' enquired Holly.

'Oh, I'm visiting an old friend,' replied Spencer who was still in shock and said the first thing that came into his head.

'I didn't know that you knew Janet,' replied Holly who was out of earshot of Janet.

'I've known her for some time,' said Spencer. This was probably the only truthful part of their brief conversation.

'Are you coming back in?' asked Holly.

'No, I have a few things to do. When will you be finished here and return home?' asked Spencer.

'I'll just be an hour,' replied Janet.

'I will see you back at home then,' said Spencer as he closed the garden gate behind him.

Spencer left Janet's house wondering if the day had arrived when everything would be exposed in the open. Holly meanwhile was greeted by Janet at the front door and the two of them walked inside the house.

'I didn't know you knew my husband,' remarked Janet.

'I don't know him,' replied Holly.

'Well you seemed to know him, because you were talking to him just a minute ago on the footpath,' insisted Janet.

'The person I was talking to on your garden footpath is my husband,' said Holly.

'No, he can't be. We both can't be married to the same man,' insisted Janet.

'There has to be some mistake,' replied Holly.

'No mistake. I'll prove that I am married to this guy,' said Janet.

She disappeared into the kitchen to make some teas and on her way back into the lounge she had picked up a wedding album, which she proudly displayed to Holly to prove her point.

Holly was stunned to see the evidence in all its reality and in her shock for a brief moment was lost for words.

'Do you mean to say that William is related to my three children?' queried Holly.

'Looks like it,' said Janet.

'It's all falling into place now. No wonder he didn't want us to continue our friendship. Wait till I see him. He will wish he had never been born by the time I've finished with him,' remarked Holly in her anger.

'Yes, he will get similar treatment from me. He always seemed to make excuses when I tried to arrange for two husbands to join us on an evening out,' replied Janet.

'This means that as Spencer married me first, you have entered into a bigamist bogus marriage with him Janet,' remarked Holly who was unaware that her circumstances on bogus marriages were no different to hers.

'Do you think we aught to involve the police? This goes down as a crime,' said Janet.

'Not yet. I'll see what he has got to say for himself first,' replied Holly.

Holly intended to stay at Janet's house a full hour, but her curiosity of why Spencer had married two women was getting the better of her and after just twenty minutes she said her farewell's to her friend and left.   When she reached home Spencer was not there, so she waited indoors pending his arrival. She didn't have to wait long because Spencer turned up clutching a bunch of flowers.

'These are for you,' he said handing her the flowers.

Holly took the flowers and threw them straight into the waste bin.

'Why did you do that?' asked Spencer.

'You have married two women, me and Janet,' said Holly.

Spencer, realised that his whole world was about to fall apart. He had no alternative than to confess that he had gone through a marriage ceremony with Janet. However, he thought it probably better not to make the situation worse by mentioning the other three wives he had married.

'But why have you done this?' asked Holly who was curious to know why he had strayed.

'I may have some difficulty in answering this question. I know I shouldn't have, but I met someone else and before I knew what was happening she was expecting my child,' replied Spencer who didn't like explaining the more intimate details of the relationship.

'You know that this is bigamy which is against the laws of the realm,' said Holly who by this stage was getting very flustered.

'What are you going to do? Are you going to inform the police?' asked Spencer who was at his wit's end.

'Surprisingly, no I am not. I realise that I am your first wife, so I am your legal true spouse whereas Janet who went through a bogus marriage is not your wife at all,' replied Holly who had calmed down from her state of anger.

Spencer thought after having been rumbled for his bad behaviour that it would be more prudent to say nothing in his defence and let Holly do all the talking. He certainly didn't want to contradict her by saying that he was married to another woman called Glenda, which made her marriage to him bogus also.

'Now Spencer, I want you to promise me that you will never see Janet again,' insisted Holly.

'That may be a little difficult because I have my daughters Vera, Xavia and Yvonne, living at Janet's address,' replied Spencer.

'That's another thing your relationship with Janet must have been pretty intense because you had three children with her,' Holly pointed out.

'Well I do love both of you,' admitted Spencer.

Holly was furious with Spencer's remark as it was bad enough sharing the man she adored but to share his affections also, was something she was finding hard to contemplate.

'Love her or not. I'm warning you Spencer, that if you make any more visits to Janet's house then you and I are finished,' threatened Holly.

Spencer, realised that he had had a lucky escape, decided that he had no alternative than to agree to Holly's terms. However, he knew that the strong affinity he had with his daughters would not allow him to ignore them, which meant that he had to continue visiting Janet's address despite the promise he had made to Holly.

'Now you must promise me something also,' insisted Spencer.

'Spencer. You are in no position to dictate terms,' said Holly who was still very angry.

'Listen to me. I don't want you calling on Janet anymore,' stressed Spencer.

'You must be joking, after this I can't stand the woman,' replied Holly.

Spencer left Holly's house on the pretence of going back to work and went straight to Janet's house. His purpose was to restrain Janet from contacting the police.

Spencer apprehensively entered the house and was immediately screamed at by Janet to leave and ushered him towards the door. Not even Spencer's protestations and apologies which were relayed in abundance softened Janet's mood of complete rejection. Janet was so upset that Spencer knew that he had to leave, but before he did he wanted to get his message across.

'Janet promise me that you will not go to the police until you have spoken to me first,' requested Spencer.

'Why should I,' replied Janet.

'Because I am your provider and if I am jailed then I can provide for you no longer,' said Spencer.

Janet didn't answer Spencer's question leaving him uncomfortably in some doubt.

'Well, I have something I want to tell you. Do you remember John, the man with whom I was once engaged?' asked Janet.

'Yes, I remember him. What about him?' replied Spencer.

'Well, I'm still seeing him,' informed Janet.

'Why?' asked Spencer who felt that his ego had been knocked for six.

'Spencer, the reason is that the three girls and I hardly ever see you and I was fed up with living such a lonely life,' replied Janet.

Spencer left Janet's house thoroughly dejected and headed for his local Portsmouth public house with thoughts of deceit by one of his wives. Casting aside all thoughts of his own deceits, he thought that he had well and truly been let down.

In the corner of the pub he found his usual seat and sipped slowly away at his pint. He was so distant with his thoughts that he didn't see another person joining him at his table. When he did recover from his state of blankness he realised that John, Janet's one time fiancé had sat at his table.

'You looked deep in thought there,' said John.

'Yes, I was miles away,' agreed Spencer.

'So you let Janet down,' said John who seemed ready to start an argument.

'Well, that is what Janet thinks,' replied Spencer.

'Tell me. Why did you marry Janet when you knew that you were already married?' asked John.

'I think you had something to do with that. You told me that if I didn't marry Janet you would come and sort me out,' replied Spencer.

'I didn't know at the time that you were already married and you said nothing on the subject. You broke up our engagement in your selfishness and ruined any chance I had of marrying Janet,' said John whose voice was rising in volume with every word that he uttered.

'Look it was you that told me Janet was pregnant and that I had to do the decent thing and marry her, which I dutifully did,' replied Spencer who was feeling uncomfortable on the way the conversation was going.

'Well I would like you to know that Janet and I are back together again. She doesn't want to turn you in. For the love of God I don't know the reason why she thinks this way, but I would say that you Spencer have had a lucky escape,' said John.

Spencer sat with his head in his hands half listening to what John was saying.

'Now, you may have thought you have got away with it with Janet, but you haven't got away with it with me,'

Spencer had had enough of his chat with John, vacated the table and walked out of the building followed closely by John. Outside Spencer was attacked from behind by John.

'I told you I would teach you a lesson,' shouted John as he laid into Spencer with a barrage of punches knocking him onto the ground. Spencer tried to get up onto his feet but was kicked in the chest dropping him back on the pavement. In the seconds that followed two passing men restrained John from applying any further damage to Spencer.

In agony Spencer rolled about on the pavement clutching at his chest.

'Do you want us to call the police,' said one of Spencer's helpers.

'No! Don't call the police,' insisted Spencer.

'Why ever not? This man has assaulted you,' said the same helper.

'The injuries I have sustained, I thoroughly deserve, so don't call the police,' pressed Spencer.

The two men helped Spencer to his feet and left him with his attacker.

'No words can describe the hatred I have for you,' said John who restrained himself from further physical attack.

'Alright. You have had your revenge. Now leave me alone,' said Spencer still holding his side.

The two men went their separate ways. Spencer walked away in the direction of Janet's house and John wandered off in the opposite direction.

When Spencer reached Janet's house he bombarded her with questions regarding her intentions towards John. However Janet was still reeling over her discovery about Holly and was not in the best mood to answer Spencer's questions.

'Listen Janet. You will have to give up John,' insisted Spencer.

'I shall do nothing of the sort. Anyway, how many women do you want?' asked Janet.

Spencer thought about the question and had no desire to answer it.

'I am not sure where I stand with you,' said Spencer.

'Well I shall tell you. I intend to marry John. It's probably something I should have done from the start. I realise now that I should never have broken the engagement off with John,' said Janet.

Spencer was stunned about hearing this and sincerely hoped that she didn't mean what she was saying.

'You feel angry at the moment, but you may feel differently tomorrow,' said Spencer whose ego had been battered by her revelation.

'The problem I am faced with Spencer is that having gone through a bogus wedding and a legitimate certificate issued to certify the event, I am not sure where I stand legally in cancelling the certificate,' said Janet.

'I'm not sure I can help you with that one. That is why I think you shouldn't go ahead with it,' insisted Spencer.

'Oh, I intend to go ahead with it alright, even if it means me going to the police,' said Janet who was clearly angered by Spencer's remarks.

'No! Don't go to the police. Nothing can be gained by you taking such a measure. There are also Vera, Xavia and Yvonne to consider. Also they may think you had something to do with the bogus marriage,' pleaded Spencer.

'My mind is made up,' insisted Janet.

Spencer, aware that he was about to be exposed, ceased trying to persuade Janet, believing that he was fighting a lost cause. The problem he had which gave him great concern, was, who was going to inform the police first? Was it going to be Janet, Karen or Holly. He didn't think that Glenda would say anything because she was the only one he was married legally to. She had nothing to gain by exposing him, but had everything to gain.

Spencer had to think of a strategy.

*

Spencer realised that in having now reached the stage where he had upset all his five wives and was virtually living the life of a recluse, he might as well speak to Jerry his employer, to see if the job that was at one time offered to him was still available. He thought it was time that he stopped driving up and down the country trying to please his partners and wanted to settle down in one place.

An arrangement to see his boss was made and Spencer turned up on time in order to pursue Jerry regarding a permanent more stable job.

'Well Spencer, you have already phoned me and told me why you wanted to see me,' said Jerry.

'That's right,' agreed Spencer, 'I did wonder whether that job you offered me earlier for the position of Transport Manager was still available,' said Spencer.

Jerry looked perplexed and rounded on Spencer who was completely taken aback.

'You've got a cheek. Turning down a generous offer I made to you some time ago and now wanting to take it at a time that is convenient to you,' replied Jerry annoyed that Spencer could even consider approaching him on the subject.

'I can appreciate you being angry but I really need that job because driving is now beginning to take its toll on me,' said Spencer.

'Well I will give you the job, however it will not be on the same terms that I offered before. This is because you need to be taught a lesson. You can have the job on the same weekly money you are receiving now, the only difference being is that you will get a company car,' replied Jerry.

This was not what Spencer wanted to hear, the offer made to him before doubled his yearly income.

However, he was in no position to argue with Jerry and accepted his new role with good grace.

Before I go into my new office to start my job, I would like to ask you a question. Now you may think that the question is strange but nevertheless I would like to see if you can answer it.

'Go on, shoot away,' said Jerry.

'Have you ever heard the term 'onomatopoeia?' asked Spencer.

'Yes, I have. It relates to a word which by sound imitates the word it is meant to describe,' said Jerry.

'Can you give me an example?' asked Spencer.

'Yes, 'meow' the sound that a cat makes is an onomatopoeia,' said Jerry who had no hesitation in giving the answer. 'I thought everyone knew that.'

'Yes everyone except me. I must be a bit of a numb brain,' said Spencer.

'Now why do you ask me that,' said a curious Jerry.

'I once picked on a headmaster of a school for expecting my son to know that word. I simply wasn't aware how universal the word is known,' replied Jerry.

Spencer retired to his new office and the first thing he did was to write 'onomatopoeia' down from a dictionary and practice the spelling of it.

Chapter 17 Jim

Spencer was travelling towards Birmingham when he received a telephone call from Jim. From the gist of the conversation it appeared that Jim wanted to urgently speak to him. Spencer thinking that it might be something to do with Karen, arranged to meet Jim in a cafe just outside Birmingham. As he was travelling towards that direction he agreed to meet Jim in the afternoon.

Jim greeted Spencer like an old friend. He couldn't believe that this was the same person who at one time physically bullied him and treated him so badly when they worked together. The transformation in Jim was astounding and Spencer wondered if there was an ulterior motive in Jim's changed attitude. He was also longing to hear what he had to say that seemed so important.

'Oh, it's good of you to see me on such short notice,' said Jim in an over friendly voice.

'Is anything wrong? Why, the urgency?' asked Spencer who was becoming suspicious.

'Well, it's like this and I'll come straight to the point. It's about the one hundred pounds a week you are paying me,' said Jim.

'I know, you don't need it anymore so you want me to cancel it,' replied Spencer.

'No! Not at all, I want you to raise it,' replied Jim.

'Raise it? It's not possible. I cannot afford to pay you any more, my wages will not run to it,' insisted Spencer who had then realised why Jim wanted to see him so urgently. He just wanted to increase his blackmailing demands.

'Look, I can't manage on what you pay me and all I want is another fifty pounds a week on top of the hundred that you already pay me,' said Jim.

'Then you will have to get it from elsewhere, because you will not get it from me, I'm paying you all I can afford,' insisted Spencer.

Spencer rose from his chair as if to leave, but was promptly restrained by a grip on the arm and told by Jim to retain his seat.

'If you don't do as I ask, then I will have no alternative than to inform the correct authorities of your bigamist activities,' Jim forcefully insisted.

'I don't think you will, because if you did, then you would lose the weekly money that you currently receive from me, simply because I won't pay out any money if I am in prison,' replied Spencer.

'Listen, I am desperate. A desperate man does desperate things. I cannot get a job and I cannot live on the money that you pay me, so if you are not going to give me any additional money then you cannot rely on me being discrete,' replied Jim.

'I have given you my answer. If you feel that you must go to the police, then you must do it because I can't release any more money to you,' insisted Spencer.

Jim's whole attitude began to change. He became angry, insulting and his whole body language indicated a man who had frustratingly not achieved is own way.

Spencer rose off his chair and walked out of the cafe, leaving Jim to ponder over his thoughts, but confident that Jim would not inform anyone of the secret they shared.

Jim realised that he had reached the limit of what Spencer could afford and was aware that if anything he had to protect his benefactor from the attention of others.

Three months later Jim managed to attend an interview for a job with a haulage company. However, he put Spencer's name down as an existing work colleague who would supply a character reference on application. Spencer was most unhappy to do this, but was conscious that if he didn't, Jim would continue to pursue him for further financial support at any time and opined that it would be better for him if his blackmailer was working.

When the time came for Spencer to assist in Jim's efforts to attain employment, he found that in writing a reference for his blackmailer, he had to falsify the qualities appertaining to Jim's character.

With Spencer's assistance, Jim finally succeeded in attaining a job.

When Spencer heard of his brother-in law's success, he approached Jim to tell him that as he had transferred his life to being a money earner, suggested that he would no longer require any further financial assistance from him.

Jim strongly disagreed and reaffirmed Spencer's commitment to continue with the weekly contributions, reminding him of the consequences should he ever fail. Spencer was furious about the sheer greed of this man and vowed to himself that if he ever did get caught for his indiscretions, he wouldn't hesitate to inform the legal authorities of Jim's blackmailing activities.

Six months later Jim had succeeded in achieving a good position within his new employment earning a higher salary than Spencer was receiving. However, even with this change of fortune, Jim never attempted to relax any part or whole of the weekly contributions he was receiving from Spencer.

Chapter 18 In Hiding

Spencer believed that as four wives knew of his bigamist activities and threats were being made to expose him, it was time to go into hiding. The first thing he had to do was to hand in his notice at work. When he did eventually pluck up the courage Jerry wasn't at all happy, having recently placed Spencer into a managerial role. However once he had satisfied Jerry that he really did intend to leave, then Spencer had considered that he had cut off all ties and was therefore free to go where he wanted and do what he wanted without being beholden to anyone.

Before Spencer went anywhere he had to buy himself a car, because the vehicle he was using belonged to the hauliers. The purchase of a cheap vehicle meant that he could travel anywhere in the United Kingdom or abroad.

Having made his purchase he headed off on the open road. He continued until he reached Blackpool where he booked into a Bed and Breakfast house. Spencer believed that in staying at this unknown address he could not be found or contacted. Initially he had requested a stay of four weeks which he could either extend or move to another location.

He used a false name of Spencer Walsh when making his booking.

The landlady was a Mrs Lorna Denver, a kindly lady in her mid thirties who was small and slim built. Spencer knew that this single woman measured up to his category of availability and therefore temptation. Knowing that he could not trust himself, he was not happy about his selection of accommodation. He kept telling himself that since he had overcome the test in Great Yarmouth of passing up beautiful women, that he had since moved on and that temptation was no longer a problem.

One week passed in the Bed and Breakfast and Spencer was beginning to live a carefree existence with very few worries. However he did miss his wives and families but hoped that his longing to see them again would pass.

There was however, one problem with his new accommodation. Lorna was becoming increasingly friendly with him. What Spencer could not understand, was that in his single days, he did all the chasing, but when he saw women as a problem and even a danger, the female gender had reverted to chasing him. Although his ego found this paradox giving him a warm feeling inside, it nevertheless created a problem for Spencer. He knew he was weak where women were concerned and realised it was going to create a big problem while he boarded there. He regarded this as a bigger test than he faced at Great Yarmouth, so in order to combat the problem, he stayed away from Lorna for as much as he could.

After two weeks in Lorna's establishment, Spencer noticed in the newspaper that he was getting media attention. Apparently Glenda had reported him missing and unfortunately there was a photograph of him within the article together with a full description of height, weight and eye colour. However it was refreshing to note that the article about him did not disclose any of his bigamist activities. Unfortunately there was no hiding the newspaper from Lorna, who immediately spotted it.

'I didn't know you were married,' said Lorna. 'It appears your wife is looking for you. Don't you think you ought to contact her and tell her where you are.'

'No! I have left home and of course it's up to me if I want to go back. I have to tell you that I have no intention to return to her,' replied Spencer.

As time was nearing the end of Spencer's booking period at the Bed and Breakfast, it was evident that Lorna was becoming more and more friendly towards him. The tactile expressions of occasionally placing her hand on his during meal times were frequently increased. Spencer gave her no encouragement, on the contrary he did his very best to avoid her. For although he considered her attractive, it was constantly on his mind that women and relationships had caused him much trouble in the past and was combination he had to avoid at all costs. He would often go out and leave Lorna on her own and return late at night after she had gone to bed.

It was the eve of the last day at the Bed and Breakfast. Spencer had gone out, as was then his usual practice. He spent his time looking round the shops, dining out and then finally ending up in a pub for some light night drinks. When he returned back at the Bed and Breakfast at approximately midnight, Lorna had retired to bed. Spencer quietly climbed the stairs, undressed, slipped into bed and turned out the light. It wasn't long before he had drifted into a deep sleep.

Meanwhile Lorna had heard Spencer moving up the staircase and heard the click of his light going off. When she thought he was asleep she crept into his bedroom and into his bed.   Spencer who by this time was comatose by drink continued in his slumber unaware that he had another person sharing his bed.

After an hour of listening to Spencer snoring and filling the air with beer fumes, Lorna thought it was time she woke him up.   After all she considered, he was no good to her in his drink fuelled state of unconsciousness.

She started to kiss his neck and the upper part of his bare torso, which had no effect because Spencer was still dead to the world.   Lorna then started to run her hands across his chest and then along the lower part of his abdomen, but still there was no response from Spencer.   Her hands wandered up and down his thigh, then across the pubic bone.   Finally she dropped her hand onto his penis which was limp and not responding in the way she wanted.   Lorna gently started to caress it, whereupon Spencer suddenly awoke startled and quickly realising that someone else was sharing his duvet jumped out the bed.   He swiftly moved over to the light switch and turned on the light. When, in his naked state he saw Lorna beneath the duvet, he quickly covered his lower body with a pillow and turned the light off to shield his embarrassment.

'What are you doing in here,' asked Spencer to the naked Lorna.

'Well I thought you could desperately do with some company,' replied Lorna who couldn't understand why Spencer had not returned to the bed.

This was the ultimate test of temptation for Spencer, but he had made up his mind that he would not succumb to Lorna's charms or enticement. He had too many reasons for keeping women at a distance and he wasn't about to fall into another trap.

'Look Lorna I am very tired, so I must ask you to leave,' requested Spencer.

Lorna remained firm in the bed.

'Why, are you gay or something?' asked Lorna who had thought that having been refused sex, she had been insulted.

'No! There have been times when maybe I wished I was gay,' replied Spencer.

'Then come back to bed and stop all this silliness,' insisted Lorna.

'I'm sorry. Believe me you have put a tremendous temptation my way. However I have come to realise, probably a bit late in life, that you cannot jump into bed with every person that you physically find attractive. It causes trouble and can sometimes bring on stress,' said Spencer.

Lorna after doing a lot of thinking slowly removed herself from the bed. In the dim moonlight Spencer could make out the silhouette of this beautifully formed body moving over to her clothes which she had placed neatly on the chair. Even at that moment Spencer's resistance was fighting the opportunity of him changing his mind. As Lorna opened the door to leave the room she turned to Spencer with a casual 'goodnight' and left.

Spencer, whose rest was interrupted, was unable to sleep during the rest of the night. His mind was on the families he had walked out on. Ever mindful that escaping was the answer to all his prayers was beginning to wonder if it was the start of a new set of problems. In essence he missed all of them.

The next morning Lorna had very little to say to him. There was an uncomfortable atmosphere in the house, for whereas at one time Spencer was always trying to avoid Lorna, the early hours of the day brought a reversal of the roles. Lorna made herself scarce and Spencer even had to go and find her to settle the boarding bill.

There was a brief goodbye and Spencer was on his way again. As his car left Blackpool, Spencer's thoughts turned to the events of the recent night. He likened it to the test he was faced with at Great Yarmouth and considered that he had indeed conquered his problem. Spencer opined that if occasions arose in the future, where he would be faced with temptation he would always be able to overcome the problem. However his thoughts turned to Glenda and thought that had he discovered the answer to his problem when he married her, he wouldn't be in the predicament that he faced.

Spencer hadn't travelled far when he saw a sign which said vacancies just outside Preston. It was a Guest House run by a Mr. Laurence Bradbury. When he rang the bell and he saw that the proprietor was a man he was delighted. . He was anxious to load his belongings into the room assigned to him, having booked his place in the Guest House for two weeks

Mr. Bradbury who liked to be called Laurie was quick to get to know his new visitor and Spencer enjoyed his company. In fact unlike Lorna's place he hardly ever left the Guest House and was content to stay in and read books, watch television in the lounge or chat to Laurie. The proprietor was about thirty five years of age, had jet black hair, approximately six feet in height and was of slim build.

'I see you live here on your own,' said the inquisitive Spencer.

'Yes, my wife left me two years ago,' replied Laurie, who really had thought he had found a new friend to talk to.

'So you are now alone. Are there any significant others?' enquired Spencer.

'Yes, I am seeing someone else. She will be coming round later on and I will introduce you to her,' replied Laurie.

'Oh, I shall look forward to that,' said Spencer.

'There is only one problem in my life. I have just received news she is expecting my child,' admitted Laurie.

'Sorry, I don't see what the problem is,' admitted Spencer.

'Well she says that she will leave me if I don't marry her and the fact is that I'm still married to the woman who left me,' said Laurie.

'Oh dear,' replied Spencer, not knowing what to say and recalling the similarities with his own problems.

'Under similar circumstances, what would you do?' asked Laurie.

'I don't think that I am the right person to ask,' replied Spencer hoping that he wasn't going to be pursued with the questions.

'You must have an opinion. For example would you wed the girl with the knowledge that you were already married?' asked Laurie.

'I was hoping you were not going to ask me that question. The answer is, if you wed this woman you will be breaking the law, as bigamy is a crime,' replied Spencer.

'So what you are saying is if you were faced with the same problem, marriage would be out of the question,' said Laurie.

'Yes, indeed.   I suppose I am saying that,' replied Spencer.

Spencer mused that here he was giving advice on avoiding bigamy, when all the time he had knowingly broken the laws applicable to this crime, not just once, but many times over. He realised that amongst his other discretions of lies and cheating, he could add hypocrisy to the list.

'So you believe that I should tell my lady friend that I cannot marry her and if that means that I lose her and never seeing my child, then so be it,' recapped Laurie.

'Yes, that is what I believe,' replied Spencer.

Spencer could see the sadness coming over Laurie's face and knew that what he had said was not what Laurie wanted to hear.

'Now I really don't know what to do,' admitted the thoroughly dejected Laurie.

'If you take my advice, you will thank me one day,' said Spencer.

'Alright when she turns up, will you have a word with her?' asked Laurie.

Spencer pondered over the question. He had now taken over the role of agony Aunt.

'Yes alright,' said Spencer reluctantly.

*

At eight o'clock in the evening, the door bell rang and Laurie was quick to answer it. Spencer remained in the lounge watching the television and Laurie disappeared with his caller which was Laurie's girlfriend.

A whole hour passed and Laurie asked Spencer to follow him into the dining room so that he could discuss the problem of marriage to the girlfriend. As they walked through, she was standing with her back to them looking out of the window. She turned around to see who had walked into the room and Spencer almost toppled over with shock. It was Lorna from the Bed and Breakfast. Lorna also acted with similar surprise.

'Do you know one another?' asked Laurie who couldn't help noticing the apparent surprise shared by the other two in the room.

'No! I've never seen this man before in my life. Who is he?' asked Lorna.

Lorna looked away to hide her embarrassment.

'I'm sorry, I'll introduce you. Spencer this is Lorna and Lorna this Spencer,' said Laurie.

With the introductions Spencer offered his hand to Lorna and she responded with the handshake.

'Laurie, I think it would be better if I spoke to Lorna alone,' suggested Spencer.

'Okay, if you think that would be better,' replied Laurie, who immediately left the room.

Spencer and Lorna were then left in the room alone in complete silence not knowing what to say to each other. The atmosphere between them became very uncomfortable.

After three agonising minutes Spencer broke the silence.

'Lorna you can't marry Laurie. Laurie appears to be a nice chap, whereas we both know that you are a player,' said Spencer.

'I don't know why you are getting involved in something that doesn't concern you,' replied Lorna.

'Believe me. I don't want to get involved. If I'd had known beforehand that you were his girlfriend I wouldn't have entertained the idea,' said Spencer.

'So what else has he wanted you to say to me, that he can't say himself?' asked Lorna.

'Well for one thing Laurie is already married, even though his wife left him two years ago. Marrying him would be an act of bigamy, which I'm sure you are aware is a crime,' advised Spencer.

'I wasn't told that he was already married. Then we will just live together,' informed Lorna.

'Have you no shame Lorna, you will jump into bed with anyone that will stay at the Bed and Breakfast. Now you want to live with this man and continue with your old ways,' said Spencer.

'I think I've had enough of this conversation, so I would ask you to leave and send Laurie back in here,' said Lorna.

Spencer left the dining room and walked into the lounge where Laurie was waiting.

'How did you get on?' asked Laurie.

'Okay, I suppose. She now knows that she can't marry you, but is happy to move in with you?' replied Spencer.

'Oh Spencer, I can't thank you enough for what you have done,' said Laurie who seemed delighted and rushed into the dining room where he gave Lorna a big hug.

Spencer had drawn similarities between Lorna and himself and thought how fortunate Laurie was not to be able to wed this woman. He mused that one day Laurie will come to the realisation that making Lorna a permanent partner would be a big mistake.

When Spencer went to leave the Guest House, Laurie refused to take any money believing that Spencer had done him a great service in sorting out his problem.

'I insist that you take the money Laurie, because one day you will realise that I had been no help to you at all,' said Spencer.

Spencer left the Guest House, leaving Laurie mystified about what he had just heard.

*

Back on the road Spencer attempted to find himself another place to stay and discovered just what he was looking for on the other side of Preston. It was a Guest House which belonged to a married couple Roy and Jackie Fellows on the edge of the town. The owners who were in their mid thirties seemed friendly enough so Spencer decided that the place was good enough to initially book himself in for a week.

Two days into his stay it was noticed that Jackie would go off to bingo, leaving Roy to chat with Spencer. The two of them seemed to be getting on very well together and had many shared interests. Then the door bell rang.

'I think you could have a customer,' remarked Spencer.

'No, it won't be a customer it will be my girlfriend calling, she always calls when Jackie has gone out,' said Roy in a matter of fact manner.

A young woman walked in who Roy introduced as Deidre who was a slim young woman approximately twenty eight years of age with green eyes. The two chatted away to Spencer for a short while and then disappeared. Spencer didn't see them again until just before Jackie returned. Deidre said her farewells to Spencer and then left. Jackie then came in completely oblivious that her husband had seen anyone during her absence.

Spencer was appalled by this behaviour and the next day when Roy was on his own he thought he would tackle his errant proprietor about his bad behaviour.

'Roy, you have a lovely wife, yet you treat her badly by having an affair with another woman,' said Roy.

'I don't think it is any of your business,' said Roy who appeared to be getting annoyed with Spencer's nosy behaviour.

'You are probably right, but surely you are open to take a bit of advice,' replied Spencer.

'A bit of advice? I expect you have done the very same thing yourself,' said Roy.

'It's not me we are discussing,' replied Spencer.

'No you're right and it's not me we are discussing either, so let's have an end to this conversation,' insisted Roy.

Spencer was disgusted that Roy should treat his wife in this way. He then began to think of his own life and realised that it was any many respects no different from Roy's. Instead it was worse, he had mistreated all his wives by embarking on one affair after another. Seeing Roy's appalling behaviour brought to his attention his own failures. He started to think that he was in no position to dictate to Roy, Lorna or anyone regarding the subject of infidelity and thought if anything he had behaved far worse in the past. However, Spencer longed to tell Jackie of her husband's affair, but thought it better to remain silent. Spencer was very much aware that silence and secrecy were the two things that protracted infidelity.

Spencer was so incensed by Roy's behaviour that he felt he couldn't stay there another day and left the Guest House early next morning. In his period of trying to escape his own problems, he felt that he had been educated on relationships and how to behave when in one. He mused that if he could turn the clock back he would certainly have approached relationships differently and directed his behaviour to that of a more caring individual.

Back on the road, Spencer headed for Birmingham as he felt it was time that he went back home. Although he had learnt a lot while he was away he saw escaping his problems as having more disadvantages than advantages. He missed his family. However angered they were with him, he had to call in and see them. Spencer was sure that Glenda who had managed to organise a press release on him as a missing person would be pleased to see him.

Money was also running out for Spencer, so the first thing he had to do was find himself a job. As he neared Birmingham he noticed a nameplate which said 'Hauliers' and thought he would call in on the chance that they would require a driver.

Seeing a worker in the car park he asked for and was directed to the Transport Manager's office. He knocked walked in and to his surprise saw Jim Walker sitting behind the desk.

'I'm surprised to see you. What do you want to see me about?' asked Jim.

'I'm equally surprised to see you. I'm enquiring if you need any drivers here?' asked Spencer.

'Why should I give you a job? You managed to get me sacked in the last one,' said Jim.

'Because you know that I am a good driver and worker,' replied Spencer.

'Well as it so happens, we have all the drivers we need,' replied Jim.

Spencer politely said 'thank you' turned around and went for the door to leave.

'Wait just a minute,' said Jim. Spencer turned around to face him.

'It's true to say that we are not looking for anyone, but I would be foolish to turn you away because if I did, you wouldn't be able to continue the weekly payments I receive off you,' explained Jim.

Jim had a rather unfortunate way of putting his words across which he did with such relish when he had something unpleasant to convey, accompanied with a distasteful grin.　　Spencer was sure that in accepting this job that he needed, he would in time live to regret taking it on under Jim's control. However, Jim did ensure that Spencer was paid good money, although even this had an ulterior motive.

The next call he had to make was Glenda who was the other side of the town.　　When Spencer reached the house, he was apprehensive regarding how he was going to be received.　　He needn't have worried because Glenda was delighted to see him and so were the four adult children Malcolm, Quilly, Norma and Patricia.

Patricia had in fact arranged to get married which received a pleasurable response from Spencer.

'Come on then tell all.　Whose the lucky fellow?' asked Spencer.

'Oh, it's someone slightly younger than me, but he's adorable,' said Patricia.

'What's his name?' enquired Spencer.

'William Evans,' said Patricia.

'Does he have a mother called Karen,' asked Spencer.

'Yes, he does, but how do you know that?' asked Patricia.

Spencer did not answer her but instead grabbed hold of Glenda's arm and took her into the kitchen where they were alone.

'Look Glenda, she can't marry her fiancé because William is Karen's boy,' pointed out Spencer.

Both Spencer and Glenda returned to the lounge.

'Sorry, Patricia you cannot marry this man. I forbid it,' insisted Spencer.

'Dad I'm not going to have you dictate to me who I can and cannot marry,' said Patricia in discontented voice.

'Tell her Glenda,' urged Spencer.

'You cannot marry William, Patricia because he is your brother,' said Glenda.

'I don't believe this. Which one of you had an affair?' asked Patricia in disbelief.

'It was your father,' said Glenda.

Patricia was furious and marched over to Spencer banging her fists on his chest and crying.

'I meet a lovely man who I want to marry and it happens to be my brother,' she said sobbing her heart out, 'How ridiculous is that?'

For Spencer things could not have got any worse. The other three children tried to comfort Patricia, but she was inconsolable.

Spencer thought it might be a good idea if he quietly left. Everyone was so upset by the news that they didn't see Spencer leaving the door. He did think of calling on Karen while he was in Birmingham and then thought it probably better that he didn't visit.

As he left his mobile phone rang; it was Jim the Transport Manager. He wanted Spencer to call into Grimsby in Lincolnshire and pick up a load. With so much bad news he had to impart in Birmingham, he was glad of the call and to be on the road again.

When Spencer arrived at the haulage yard he was met by William who had been waiting for him. With all the problems he was carrying in his head, William was the last person he wanted to see.

Apparently Patricia had heard the telephone call on the mobile phone regarding Spencer heading back to the yard and called William.

'Hello Dad, you're just the person I wanted to see,' said William as Spencer climbed out of his cab.

'I think I have a pretty good idea of why you want to see me,' replied Spencer.

'How is it that you can mess up my life in this way?' asked William.

'Listen William. You cannot marry your half sister, it is against the law,' replied Spencer.

'Mum has told me that you entered a bigamist relationship with her, I suppose you are going to tell me that you didn't break the law,' said William who was beginning to raise his voice.

'I have broken the law, but two wrongs do not make a right,' replied Spencer.

'I completely blame you for this mess,' insisted William.

'Well I partly blame your mother,' said Spencer trying to defend himself. 'I can remember a day as youngster's when you and Patricia were playing in Glenda's back garden.'

'Yes, but that was only on one occasion. While we were growing up we had no further contact and as we have different surnames there was no thought that we were related,' explained William.

'I've thought about this and if I did marry her, according to the official records there is nothing to show that we are related, it is only you, mum and Glenda who knows that we are blood relatives,' said William.

Spencer thought about what William had said and realised that in order to stop this incestuous relationship, he would have to expose his own crime of bigamy. He had one trump card left which he knew would upset William but nevertheless had to play.

'Patricia might be old enough to get married you are only seventeen years of age which puts you below the age of consent. You will therefore need to seek my approval before you embark on marriage to anyone and in this particular instance, I am not prepared to give it,' insisted Spencer.

William was furious and stormed off in the direction of the exit gate, leaving Spencer wondering if the brief altercation would inflame his son sufficiently to go to the police.

Spencer had become concerned and decided to climb back into his cab and head off towards Janet's house with a view to obtaining Karen's help in putting a stop to the marriage between William and Patricia.

Janet was in no mood to speak to Spencer about anything and initially would not allow him into the house. Following an argument at the door Spencer managed to convince Karen to discuss the problem that plagued his mind. She finally allowed him into the house on the condition that he had to be quick about what he had to say and then leave.

'I want to talk to you about the problem regarding William and Patricia,' said Spencer.

'Yes, I've just heard. I'm as shocked about it as you are,' replied Karen.

'Well what are we going to do. I've already told him that I will block any marriage between them, although when he reaches the age of eighteen, he can do as he likes,' explained Spencer.

'Well I think it's a bit late for all that because Patricia is three months pregnant. Didn't you know?' asked Karen.

'No! I did not,' replied Spencer who was completely shocked. 'I blame you for all this Karen.'

'I thought you might say that, well you can just remove yourself from this house,' replied Karen who was not going to take the blame for anything.

As Spencer left Karen's house he was beginning to see how he had failed his children as a parent and mused that if he had his life over again he would have run it differently.

*

After seeing Karen, Spencer worried all the following day about the relationship between William and Patricia. He decided that he had to speak to Patricia. It was something he had to do very quickly. However like many of the other members of the family, she was not pleased to see him and tried to stop him entering the house.

'Patricia I have to speak to you,' he said as he jammed his foot in the door.

'There is nothing I want to hear from you Dad. Please go away,' she yelled.

'But it's important. You must let me in,' he remonstrated.

Patricia reluctantly released the door and let Spencer in.

'I must speak to you about William. You must give him up,' insisted Spencer.

'I will do nothing of the sort,' replied Patricia.

'Look Pat, I know about the baby, Karen informed me,' said Spencer.

'Well there's nothing you can do about that,' said Patricia.

'Listen Pat you must have the foetus aborted. You cannot have a child with your half brother,' indicated Spencer.

'Well you can forget about trying to persuade me on that one,' replied Patricia who was becoming more and more angry the longer the conversation went on.

'Look, not only is it morally wrong, there is also a health risk to the infant. Interbreeding can produce abnormalities in the infant,' pointed out Spencer.

'Dad, what I think you are really worried about is saving your own skin,' indicated Patricia.

'That's true but I am more concerned about the situation between you and William that's developing here,' insisted Spencer.

'Dad I really must ask you to leave,' insisted Patricia.

Spencer did as he was told realising that whatever he said he was not going to get through to the intransigent Patricia who was firmly standing her ground.

Chapter 19 A Visit to Blackpool

Spencer had just finished his work for the day when he received a telephone call at five o'clock in the afternoon that he was required to pick up a load at Blackpool to be delivered next day to Richmond, just west of London. This was bad news for Spencer because he had arranged to call on Iris, who he then had to cancel. He was furious and believed this to be Jim again trying to exact as much inconvenience on him as he could. This seemed to be a recurrence of the old days when Jim Walker was working for Jerry.

Although the drive was free of traffic, Spencer didn't arrive in Blackpool until just after eight o'clock. He picked up his load as arranged and then was looking for somewhere to stay the night. Spencer remembered Laurie Bradbury the Preston Guest House proprietor he stayed with the last time he visited Blackpool. This was only twenty five minutes travelling distance from his pickup point. He thought that Laurie was bound to be pleased to see him after the agony aunt help he gave the last time at the Guest House.

However when Laurie answered the door the reaction was not as Spencer had envisaged. He didn't seem at all pleased to see Spencer, but nevertheless invited him indoors. Immediately Laurie went on the offensive.

'You've got a cheek coming back here,' said Laurie.

'I really don't know what you mean,' replied Spencer who was confused about Laurie's aggressive approach.

'You didn't tell me you already knew Lorna,' said Laurie.

'No you're right I didn't. Well, it's true during my stay at the Guest House, I did meet her before she arrived here. However I never knew her that well. I merely stayed at the Bed and Breakfast that she ran,' admitted Spencer.

'Well you knew her well enough to get into bed with her,' replied Laurie in a raised voice.

'That's not what happened. She actually crept in the bedroom that I was sleeping in, during the middle of the night. The first I knew about it was when I woke up and saw her lying next to me,' remonstrated Spencer.

'I don't believe a word of what you say,' replied Laurie who was getting very annoyed with Spencer's responses.

It appeared odd to Spencer that whenever he told lies people seemed to believe him, but whenever he told the truth he couldn't convince anyone of his honesty. This was one of those occasions where candour was not being effective and frustration was taking over.

'I gather from this conversation that she has left you Laurie,' said Spencer.

'Yes! How did you know that?' replied Laurie.

'Oh, it's easy to see what has happened here Laurie. Lorna wanted a way out and is using me as an excuse,' suggested Spencer.

'Do you really think that is what happened?' enquired Laurie.

'I'll tell you what I think happened. Lorna had a big row with you and in order to escalate the argument so that you wouldn't try and pursue her to get her back, she fabricated a story about me, thereby making you believe that there was a romantic affair going on with another man,' explained Spencer.

'That's exactly what happened. How did you work that one out?' asked Laurie who had calmed down.

'It really didn't take a lot of working out. In fact it is the standard 'way out' remedy used by all players. Effective isn't it?' said Spencer.

'Yes, it had me fooled alright,' replied Laurie.

'I knew she wasn't the one for you,' said Spencer in trying to make Laurie feel better about himself.

'Thanks mate, I see it all now. I think I've had a lucky escape. I suppose you want to stay here the night,' said Laurie.

'Well that was my original intention,' replied Spencer.

It seemed wherever Spencer went he was giving out advice. Although the advice given was often useful and helpful, he never adopted the tactics he offered to other people.

Spencer stayed the night and the following day he was up and six o'clock in the morning and back on the road again.

*

On the journey back from Preston, he had to drop off his load at Richmond and then call in the bank at Portsmouth regarding his ever increasing debt.

The bank wanted to see him about his escalating overdraft. Full of nervousness he was guided by a bank tiller to the Bank Manager's door. He was asked to sit in the chair and informed that the Bank Manager Harold Winters would be with him shortly.

Spencer waited patiently for fifteen minutes. The longer he waited the more nervous he became. Then suddenly the door opened and in walked this big man. Spencer couldn't believe his eyes when he noticed it was Holly's father. He knew Holly's father was a Bank Manager but didn't know that he was in charge of the bank that he used. Neither did he know the name of Holly's father which was Winters.

'What are you doing here Spencer Butcher?' asked Winters seeing his son-in-law sitting in the chair.

'You asked to see me,' said Spencer.

'Was it on a personal matter regarding you and Holly?' asked Winters.

'No I think you wanted to see me regarding my account with the bank,' replied Spencer.

'I don't recall that. In fact I don't think you are even on our books, he said as he scanned the monitor of his computer. No there's no record of you here. Are you sure you belong to this bank?' enquired Winters.

'Definitely,' assured Spencer.

'Just a minute, our records may not be up to date,' said Winters and called one of the Bank Tillers for assistance, who Winters immediately confronted.

'Spencer here, said that he has an appointment with the Bank, and I have no record of it,' said Winters. The tiller walks round the desk to view the monitor.

'Yes, there it is Spencer Andrews,' said the Bank Tiller and looking at Winters as if he had gone crazy.

'Okay, I missed that one. Leave it with me,' said Winters. The Bank Tiller left the office.

'I see it all now. You married my daughter Holly using a false name. No wonder I can't find you on our records. Now why did you do that,' asked Winters.

'You must know why I did it. Holly must have told you that I was deep in debt. I used the false name to escape debt detection when I joined your bank,' explained Spencer.

'Then why did you marry my daughter if you were in so much debt,' said Winters as he erupted into a rage.

'Well in a way you had something to do with that Sir. Because Holly was carrying your grandchild you insisted that I marry her,' explained Spencer.

'What! You nasty little person. I never liked you and I never wanted anyone like you as a son-in-law. Get out of my office,' shouted Winters.

Spencer rose from his chair as if about to leave.

'No! Sit down again. We haven't discussed why we wanted to see you,' shouted Winters who was getting really rattled by Spencer's presence.

Winter's looked again at his computer monitor banging erratically at the buttons on his keyboard.

'Now I see why you have been asked to come and see me. You are overdrawn to the tune of approximately seven thousand pounds,' observed Winters.

Although Spencer was horrified at meeting Holly's father and discovering him as the Bank Manager, in his mind he could see a way of turning it to his advantage.

'So what are you going to do about this overdraft?' asked Winters.

'Well, I put the same question to you,' said Spencer.

'I don't follow you,' replied Winters who had calmed down.

'Well, I see it this way. If I haven't any funds in the bank, I cannot provide for your daughter. I'm sure you wouldn't want her to go unfed,' explained Spencer.

'That's a form of blackmail,' said Winters.

'Is it? I see it as a necessity and a call for help directed towards a doting father,' said Spencer.

Winters's face reddened up and suddenly he was lost for words.   Spencer waited for him to say something as he pondered over what he had heard.

'Right,' he said,   'I am going to open an account in the name of Spencer Butcher.   The account in the name of Spencer Andrews will be closed.   I will put ten thousand pounds in the account out of my own money and the debt in the account of Andrews will be closed again using my own money to clear the debt.   Now have you any other debt?,' asked Winters.

Spencer realised that he had the upper hand and was determined to take advantage of it.

'Yes, as a matter of fact I have,   I have a loan of twelve thousand pounds,' admitted Spencer.

'My goodness, you sure know how to spend money,' remarked Winters.

'Okay, give me the name, address and telephone number of the Lender and I will deal with them direct,' said Winters.

Spencer did has he was asked.

'Now get out of my office, because this is the last time you will get any money from me. And another thing don't tell Holly anything about this,' yelled Winters whose anger had returned.

Spencer left the office with a smile on his face thinking to himself, *'now that is what I call a good day at the bank, I'm so glad they had the forethought to call me in.'*

Holly was expecting Spencer to call in and see her after he had been to the bank. It seemed that the problem of her finding out about Janet had all been forgotten.

After greeting Spencer, Holly asked him how he got on in the bank.

'Oh, very well. Bank Managers are not the ogres you think they are,' remarked Spencer.

'I don't know about that. If you were in my dad's bank you wouldn't have been treated quite so friendly. Dad doesn't trust anyone. He loathes clients being in debt and has a special way of dealing with them. In fact you are very fortunate not to belong to Dad's bank,' said Holly.

With his new found wealth, courtesy of Holly's father Harold Winter's, Spencer was able to treat Holly and the three children Olga, Richard and Stanley, who were all in their early twenties, to a an expensive meal in a local restaurant.

Spencer stayed the night at Holly's house and early next morning he was back on the road.

Chapter 20 Meeting Zoe

Spencer had delivered a load to Birmingham from Grimsby and stopped at a roadside cafe for a brief snack. The cafe was packed with other lorry drivers, none of whom Spencer knew. A woman aged approximately thirty five years of age walked in and he noticed that all the eyes of the cafe diners were directed towards her. This was not surprising because she oozed sex appeal with her slim figure, blue eyes and fair hair.

This lady looked totally out of place in this all male environment and from her mannerisms started to look uncomfortable as if in some way she had made a mistake by entering this 'all driver's domain'. Seeing an empty chair opposite Spencer, she walked slowly over, drew it away from the table and sat down. Now in the past Spencer would have seized the initiative with both hands and wouldn't have hesitated to make a play for this beautiful young woman. However he had enough problems and was not at all happy that temptation was put his way by her coming to his table. He considered that he had already passed the tests in Great Yarmouth and Blackpool, so he didn't relish the idea of being put to the same difficult type of trial.

He bent down to pick up his case and opened it to retrieve his newspaper, but realising that he hadn't bought one that day, gently closed it and returned the case to the side of his chair.   He was still waiting for his food and didn't know what to do with himself.   The last thing he wanted was to get into conversation with this lady.   In order to avoid any conversation with this woman, he directed his gaze to the bare walls in the room, looking at anything rather than her.   Spencer was already magnetised by the stunning appearance of this woman, but told himself that he would not be drawn in any way by her charms.   In the silence that was going on between them, the woman was observing the odd but uncomfortable behaviour of her table companion and thought she ought to speak out.

'I'm sorry, I should have asked if I could sit here,' said the woman.

'No, you are alright,' replied Spencer, who did not look at her while he was speaking.

'You seem very fidgety.   Are you uncomfortable with women around you?' asked the woman.

'Oh, take no notice of me, I'm just a bit shy,' replied Spencer.

'I think that is sweet. Normally men are trying to get off with me, and after the last decade of hearing the same cheesy chat up lines, I'm beginning to get fed up with it, so it's refreshing to come across a man who is different,' said the woman.

Spencer thought about what the woman had said, knowing that at one time he was amongst those she had so aptly described and made no attempt to answer her. However he had unknowingly developed a new tactic of shyness which was a virtue that some women like.

'Look,' she said as she looked around her, 'I'm unhappy about sitting in here with all these leering men. Can you direct me to another eating house?' said the woman.

'Yes, there is a restaurant about half a mile from here, but you will have to turn off the main road, do a left and then a right by the post office and………,' said Spencer who was stopped in his directions, by the woman putting her hand on his arm.

'Look, I am hopeless on directions, will you allow me to drive you there and you can tell me which way to go,' said the woman.

'Sorry, I've ordered some food and I'm still waiting for it,' replied Spencer.

'I will pay for the food you ordered and bring you back to your lorry. However, one thing is for sure, I cannot eat here,' insisted the woman as she looked around her.

Spencer reluctantly agreed and the two of them drove off in her car to the restaurant Spencer had recommended. The woman pulled up outside the restaurant and Spencer opened the car door for her to get out.

'A gentleman with manners, I am impressed,' said the woman as they walked into the restaurant.

The two found a table and settled into their seats. At this moment Spencer was still determined not to get involved with this woman whom he had briefly met and didn't even know her name.

'Well, I must say that you are not a very good conversationalist,' remarked the woman.

'Like, I said, I'm very shy around women,' replied Spencer determined not to get too friendly.

'We will soon put a stop to that,' the woman said with a smile, 'my name is Zoe. What is yours?'

'They call me Spencer.'

'Well Spencer, I know what you do for a living, but why are you still a single man?' asked Zoe.

'Who said I was a single man?' asked Spencer.

'Well you can't be married because your shirt hasn't been ironed and you seem too shy to even want to talk to a woman, so I think you would find it difficult to find anyone,' replied Zoe.

'What about you? Are you married?' asked Spencer.

'No, I have never married. I have never met anyone I would like to have a lasting relationship with,' replied Zoe.

The meal arrived and the two diners were locked in conversation. Spencer, without realising it had succumbed to the charms of Zoe and adopted his usual patter of the days gone by, which had proved so successful with his past conquests. By the time they had left the restaurant they had swapped telephone numbers and Spencer was in possession of Zoe's home address.

Spencer couldn't wait to see this woman again. He made regular telephone calls to Zoe and made sure that he was in Birmingham more often than he should have been. After the two of them had seen each other for six weeks, they started love making. Spencer viewed their sexual exploits as the best sexual experiences he had had in his entire life and he wasn't prepared to let her go in a hurry.

Six months into the relationship, Spencer was seeing Zoe less frequently. Then one day when he was dropping a load off to a warehouse in Birmingham he called into Zoe's home.

To Spencer's shock, Zoe was very badly ill. She had lost a lot of weight, had blurred vision, a high temperature, was short of breath and had large lumps on her neck.

'Have you got the flu?' asked Spencer as he bent down and kissed her.

'No, I have just had a doctor come round and see me. I have human immunodeficiency virus,' confirmed Zoe.

'Oh, that's alright then, I thought you had caught a nasty dose of influenza,' said Spencer with a smile.

'No, instead I've caught a nasty dose of HIV,' replied Zoe.

'What?' said a startled Spencer as the smile immediately disappeared from his face. The full realization of Zoe's illness had hit him as he understood the acronym given to him better than the full medical term. He pounded up and down the bedroom wondering what to do and say next.

Zoe's illness was a disease which spreads with sexual contact. Spencer was aware that he could also be in possession of this infection and therefore could not take the chance of passing this onto his wives.

'How do you think you caught this?' asked Spencer who was keen to know that she was not having an affair with someone else.

'It can only be a time when I was enjoying a holiday in Crete. I met a local waiter to whom I was attracted and we started seeing each other,' confided Zoe.

'You never told me about that,' said a concerned Spencer.

'No I didn't, because it was before I met you,' replied Zoe.

'You look terrible,' remarked Spencer who noticed blotches that had appeared on her skin.

'I know I do. There is a very good chance that this will develop into acquired immune deficiency syndrome,' remarked Zoe, who was struggling for breath.

'What is that?' asked Spencer.

'AIDS,' replied Zoe.

Spencer went pale with shock after hearing the abbreviated letters forming the acronym of this other disease which is a term he was more familiar with.

'Don't you see, I could die from this,' said Zoe.

Spencer was distraught at hearing these words, he didn't know what to say or how he could console his partner.

Then Zoe broke the silence.

'Let's get married,' said Zoe. Then if I do die I can pass this house onto you.

Spencer was lost in thought, believing that if he did get married, then Zoe could provide him with some financial sustainability and maybe wipe out some of his debt.

'Alright then we will do it,' said Spencer.

This time Spencer made all the arrangements. He booked the church, arranged the reception and even ordered the wedding dress for his bride. By this time the expectant groom was becoming rather blasé about marriage and viewed it as a necessity to progress the benefits in life, rather than flagrant abuse of the legal system.

The marriage was set for a June wedding, but six months prior to the important date, Spencer started to feel unwell. He developed a high temperature and was struggling to breath. Realising that it was the same symptoms that Zoe was showing, he resigned himself to the fact that he also may have contacted HIV. Zoe also was deteriorating badly. The doctor had given her the news she was dreading that she had developed AIDS from the HIV virus.

The worsening health of the intended bride and groom did not put both of them off from getting married. It was their intention that arrangements would go ahead as planned no matter how badly ill health was dragging them down.

Spencer viewed his illness as just retribution for the way that he had treated the other women in his lives. He therefore prepared himself for all the discomforts his illness would deal him in the future as well as his ultimate death.

Chapter 21   Karen's Revenge

Spencer was not keeping up with his promised visits to see his son William.   Although William partly heeded the advice of his father regarding his schooling, he was nevertheless upset that he was constantly let down. Arrangements would be made to meet William although not always kept by Spencer.   Unfortunately although Spencer tried to do his best to keep scheduled arrangements, his work and visits to other families often interrupted his calls to see William.   This aggravated and annoyed Karen.

Karen was determined to achieve her revenge on Spencer in the worst possible way she knew how. By calling the police she could invoke the maximum pain on Spencer and at the same time teach him a lesson he would never forget.   However before the revengeful Karen could exercise her quest with maximum venom, she sought the advice of her brother Jim Walker.

Jim was very protective of his provider Spencer and Karen couldn't understand why he had changed his view of the man she detested so much.   However, Karen was not aware that Jim was blackmailing

Spencer. If she did have knowledge of this, she might have had a better understanding on why Jim didn't have a bad word to say about him.

'Jim, at one time you couldn't stand the man, now you see him as a good person who has done no wrong,' said Karen.

'Karen, I'm not the sort of person to hold a grudge. I think he has proved himself to be a good husband and he absolutely adores William,' replied Jim.

'Are you mad, he keeps breaking appointments to see William, and as for being a good husband, well I can only say that he has let me down so often,' insisted Karen.

'I still think you ought to think twice about inviting the police to delve into your marriage with Spencer, after all, they may think you had something to do with it and arrest you as well,' said Jim.

'No I have made up my mind,' insisted Karen.

Karen went across to the telephone to make the call to the police, closely followed by Jim who put his hand on hers restraining her from picking up the phone.

'Look Karen, leave it a day. You are very angry at the moment, you may feel differently in the morning,' said Jim.

Jim left Karen's house and phoned Spencer and told him of Karen's intentions.

'I don't know why you are phoning me Jim. What do you expect me to do about it?' said Spencer.

'Well you could at least speak to her and try to persuade her that it would be foolish to phone the police, because she could lose the allowance she gets from you,' Jim pointed out.

'No Jim. I feel that is your job to do that. What do you think I'm paying you for?' replied Spencer.

Jim didn't like the idea of the responsibility of keeping Karen away from the police but knew that this was a job he had to do. Mindful of Spencer's words that he could lose the payments being made to him he had to do all he could to protect his benefactor.

The following day Jim returned to Karen's house to have another go at trying to persuade her not to involve the police. However, it was too late.

Karen had already phoned them and they were on their way to see her.

Jim was dumbfounded and didn't know what to say. He felt that his whole world was about to fall apart. He was aware that Spencer would stop the payments, but more importantly would his blackmailing activities come to the notice of the police.

Early in the afternoon Detective Inspector Hallet and Police Officer Foster arrived and took detailed statements from Karen in front of Jim. They wanted to know the dates when she was married and when she first became aware that Spencer had another wife.

'Now tell me,' said Hallet, 'were you aware that this was a bogus marriage?'

'Of course not. If I had known, I wouldn't have gone ahead with it,' insisted Karen.

'So where is your partner now?' asked Hallet.

'I've no idea, I expect he is on the road somewhere. He is a lorry driver,' said Karen.

'Can you give me the surname adopted when you were married,' asked Hallet.

'Evans. I truly believed that was his real name,' replied Karen.

'Thank you, that's all we need for now we will get in touch,' advised Hallet who scribbled down a few notes.

The two police officers left. Jim in the meantime had his head in his hands believing that it was only a matter of time before the crime he committed would be discovered, believing that the chances of Spencer not releasing this information would be very slim.

Chapter 22 Spencer's Illness

Spencer had been experiencing a fever for some time and decided that it was time for him to be visiting the Doctor.   The Doctor arranged for a nurse to take some blood samples and asked Spencer to return to the Surgery within fourteen days, which he duly did.

'I'm afraid I have some bad news for you Mr Andrews.   I have to inform that you are suffering from the advanced level of HIV,' reported the Doctor.

'Yes, I thought I may be,' replied Spencer.

'You don't appear too surprised,' said the Doctor.

'No, the reason is that I have been in contact with someone else with the same complaint,' replied Spencer.

'I assume this person is not your wife,' said the Doctor.

'No, you're right she isn't my wife,' answered Spencer.

'Well in that case, we will have to give a blood test to your wife and any other sexual partners you have had,' insisted the Doctor.

Spencer thought for a while and realised that the Doctor's suggestion included, Glenda, Holly and Iris and wondered how he was going to tell them that there was a possibility that they could be HIV infected, these being the only wives he had slept with since meeting Zoe. This was going to be extremely difficult because none of them knew about Zoe or the illness that she had, but they would soon know everything. Spencer was wary about telling any of the women but knew that for health reasons they all had to be informed and checked out.

As Glenda seemed to take the news that he was a bigamist better than Karen did, he thought he would try her with his revelation first, so he made arrangements that he would call. He thought that before venturing into what he thought might be a difficult exchange of words, he would stop off at the florists first and buy a bunch of flowers.

When he did arrive at the house Glenda appeared to be in a bad mood which was created by arguments with her grown up children. Spencer noticed that she was on her own; all the children being at work.

'You seem to be having a bad day my love. Maybe this will put you in a good mood,' said Spencer handing her the flowers.

'Oh, that's a lovely gesture. You never buy me flowers. What has brought this on?' asked Glenda.

Spencer ignored Glenda's question and thought it better to get everything in the open as soon as possible.

'Glenda, I have just been to the Doctor and it has been confirmed that I have a life threatening illness,' said Spencer trying to ease himself into the conversation before making his shocking disclosure.

'Oh dear, you poor thing. Is there anything I can do?' asked a concerned Glenda, her eyes welling up with tears.

'Yes, there is. Go and see the Doctor yourself and ask him to do a blood test,' said Spencer.

'Why have you acquired something that is contagious,' asked Glenda.

'Yes I have. I have been diagnosed as HIV positive,' informed Spencer waiting for Glenda to go into a rage.

'But you can only get HIV if you have injected yourself with a defective needle, had a blood transfusion with infected blood or obtained the virus through sexual contact,' said Glenda.

Spencer waited silently for Glenda to reach her own conclusion on how he had managed to contact the disease. Then suddenly she had come to the full realisation of what she was faced with.

'That's it. You have been sexually active with someone who is HIV positive,' said Glenda who had worked herself up into a frenzy.

'Calm down. All you have to do is go and see the Doctor. He will ask you to take a blood test. You may be lucky. You may have not caught it at all,' assured Spencer.

'Lucky! Do you call this luck?' shouted Glenda.

'Look Glenda it is essential that you see him,' said Spencer who was trying to calm Glenda down.

'Get out! I never want to see you again,' shouted Glenda. 'And you can take these with you.' She then picked up a vase with the flowers that Spencer had bought and threw them with full force at him. The vase hit him on the back of the head. By the time she had said the words 'get out', Spencer had turned and made for the door. As he left he could feel blood trickling down the back of his neck.

The next one to see was Holly. It was a long drive from Birmingham to Portsmouth but Spencer knew that it was important to do it even though he was not in the peak of health.

He arrived at approximately three o'clock and thought that having learnt from his last bad experience, buying flowers was perhaps not a good idea after all. He decided that nothing could be gained by buying any gift. However one thing was in Spencer's favour, because the children, Olga, Richard and Stanley were still at work.

He approached Holly in the same way that he approached Glenda using the same introductory rhetoric. However, Holly was quicker to come to a conclusion on Spencer's exploits than Glenda and in the same manner was quickly shown the door.

After such a long drive Spencer had spent only 10 minutes in Holly's house. His next task was to make his way from Portsmouth to Torbay to inform Iris of the problem.

When he arrived at Torbay it was about nine o'clock in the evening so Spencer decided to kill a bit of time in the Town until he thought the time was right when the children Thomas and Ursula had gone to bed.

At ten o'clock he entered the house. Iris was overjoyed to see Spencer and couldn't wait to tell him of her good news.

'Spencer, I have managed after all this time to sell the Manor. This means that we will have a bit more money between us. It also means that I will need your help to find another house,' said Iris brimming over with delight.

Iris was on such a high that Spencer thought that it would be a shame to bring her back to reality with the awful news he had to impart. Nevertheless, Spencer was aware that it had to be done and it was better that Iris was warned sooner, rather than later. So Spencer revealed to her the dreadful truth about Zoe and himself and sat in a chair waiting for Iris's mood to change. Iris went ballistic, throwing cups and saucers in his direction with enormous force and accuracy. It was all Spencer could do but dodge them. The missiles were coming so thick and fast that he was forced back towards the door. When

Iris had exhausted her supply of crockery, she came towards Spencer shoving him with both her hands, at the same time yelling obscenities at him at the top of her voice.

The next thing Spencer knew was that he was being pushed out of the door. As he hit the night air he could hear Iris bolting the door so as to prevent his further entry. Then everything went silent.

Spencer realised that he had now upset nearly all of his wives and that he was not welcome in any of his homes in Birmingham, Portsmouth or Torbay. The only one he hadn't upset was Linda who had died. He wondered if Linda would have approved of his shocking behaviour had she been alive and came to the conclusion that she would have accepted anything that Spencer had done no matter how bad.

Six weeks passed and Spencer was keen to know the results of the blood tests of Glenda, Holly and Iris had taken. A phone call to each of them revealed that the results had come back negative. Spencer heaved a sigh of relief that he had not passed on his problems to the ones he most cared about in his life even, though he knew that this time he had gone too far. He also feared that any homely chats and evenings out with any of the five wives was now a thing of the past.

The only thing he could do now was settle down and make a life with Zoe.

Chapter 23 An unwelcome visitor

The difficulties imposed by Jim Walker, who was not only his blackmailer and boss, were taking their toll on Spencer, so he decided to approach Jerry to see if he could get his old job back.   Jerry was delighted to see him again.   It appeared that since Spencer's departure he was missed terribly and Jerry was only too pleased to give him his old job back as Transport Manager.

'I knew you couldn't work for Walker for long and thought that one day you would return,' said Jerry.

Spencer settled into his returned position of Transport Manager and because of his vast knowledge of the haulage business was able to progress his role in the office without very little advisory assistance.   Jerry who was happy to pass the responsibility to anyone who would take it, was always extremely pleased with the way that Spencer was able to conduct the work schedules and control the drivers.

Although everything seemed to be going well without any difficulties under the guise of Spencer's control, there was one constant problem which just would not go away.   Spencer's illness was getting progressively worse. Red blotches were increasing in number on his skin, he constantly ached all over and he was coughing a lot. As he didn't share an office with anyone else, nobody was aware how badly he had deteriorated or even aware that he had a life threatening illness.

Then one day he received a knock on his door and a heavily built man walked in the office dressed in a pinstripe suite. At the time Spencer was heavily engaged in juggling the drivers work schedule for the following week. Spencer aware that someone was standing in front of his desk looked up at the visitor and almost fell off his chair with shock. It was Holly's father, Harold Winters. Before Spencer could say any words of welcome, Holly's father placed his hands on the desk and leaned forward so that his face was about three hundred millimetres from Spencer's.

'I've been looking for you. With Holly's help I was told you were here,' said Winters in an angered voice.

'What do you want from me?' said a nervous Spencer who was ready to spring into action if the occasion arose.

'I want to know why you entered into a bigamous marriage with someone whilst married to my daughter and tried to give her HIV,' asked Holly's father whose voice had entered fever pitch.

'Well, I wish I knew the answer regarding the bigamous marriage. With regard to HIV, I never tried to give her the disease, because there was a time when I didn't know I had it' replied Spencer.

'I now understand that she has been tested and has the all clear, so there is nothing more to worry about,' continued Spencer.

'There are times when I wished that you had never married my daughter,' shouted Winters.

'Well in a way you did push me into it,' replied Spencer.

'I did nothing of the sort, besides you could easily have said 'No',' said Winters.

Spencer realised that it was pointless arguing with this man who had at one time been forceful in his approach for Holly not to have children outside of the marriage, and therefore moved to the second part of the question put to him.

'I ought to pick you up and bounce you against that wall for what you have done to my little girl,' threatened Holly's father who was not convinced by Spencer's comment.

'There is no need to apply any physical violence on me, because when this illness finally kills me, your revenge towards me will be complete,' replied Spencer.

'I'm warning you Spencer, just stay clear of my daughter,' threatened Winters.

'It's true, you don't look at all well. Let's hope the end of your days will be sooner rather than later,' said the unsympathetic father of Holly.

Holly's father believing that nature would eventually take its course with Spencer, left without even saying 'goodbye' to him. Spencer meanwhile was happy that no physical violence was applied to him by his unwelcome visitor. However the intrusion did have an effect on his mind. He was unable to complete his driver's work schedule or concentrate on the remaining duties he had set himself for the day. With so many things plaguing his mind he tidied his desk and left work early.

Having been reminded of the dreadful way he had treated Holly, Spencer wondered if marrying Zoe was a good idea after all. He made a quick contact with his bride to be, who assured him that nothing could be gained by either of them being single, because marriage offered companionship and financial stability to both of them.

It was agreed then, that the marriage between them would go ahead as planned. Zoe would invite her brother and as many guests of her choosing. The wedding was arranged to be held in the local church in Zoe's home town of Birmingham.

Chapter 24 Marriage to Zoe

The Church was about to receive many guests, none of whom would know the groom. The best man was Zoe's brother who had never met Spencer before.

The stage was set for a wedding and honeymoon that would be remembered, where no expense was spared.

Spencer was first at the church and was soon met by Zoe's brother. After a handshake and a few brief words, the pair walked into the church and sat silently in the front pew waiting for the guests to arrive. No words were spoken between them.

It wasn't long before the church was filled up with chattering guests many of whom tried to get a glimpse of the groom they had never met. Some even came over to shake Spencer's hand although in reality they were trying to find out more about this mysterious man who Zoe had met and was about to marry. Spencer was always guarded with his answers and never forward in providing information about himself.

The bride wore a white wedding dress, the train of which was supported with four bridesmaids dressed in green velvet outfits. The scene was set for a very glamorous and extravagant marriage.

Spencer, who used to be very nervous during his wedding services, was so used to the formalities of the ceremony, that he had adopted a completely relaxed composure of calmness and sat in his seat anxious for the ceremony to commence.

In the meantime Detective Inspector Hallet had made a visit to Karen to establish more information about her marriage to Spencer and attain additional details regarding her discovery about the bigamy that had been committed.

'Okay, I think I have all the information I need from you for the moment, however I may be back,' said Hallet.

'Alright I'll give you all the help I can,' said Karen.

'Where will I find him now?' asked Hallet who was referring to Spencer.

'I would try the local church,' said Janet who liked to provide the odd amusing anecdote.

However on that comment the two law enforcers were on their feet and marching for the door.

'Come on Foster lets go!' said Hallet as he made a rush to get out of the house quickly followed by Foster.

'I was only joking,' said Karen as the two policemen left.

However neither of the two men had heard Karen's last comment and headed straight for the nearest church. When they arrived, they witnessed a wedding ceremony taking place which had not long begun.

As the groom turned his head to give the responses to his bride, Hallet noticed that it was Spencer Andrews, the person they were looking for. Karen, who in her deliberation to make a joke of her situation, had no idea that in an attempt to make the police officers laugh, she had unwittingly directed them to another of Spencer's weddings.

The two men found some empty pews and sat down, ready to pounce on Spencer at the earliest opportunity.

The question proffered by the priest that had always in the past gave Spencer a short heart stopping period was then directed at the congregation. By this time Spencer had become familiar with the question and overcame his nervous behaviour.

'Does any person here present, know any just cause or impediment why these two should not be joined in holy matrimony, let him now speak or forever hold his peace.'

There was the usual short pause, then a voice came booming from the church.

'Yes, I have a just cause why this marriage should not go ahead,' said Hallet stepping from the pews into the aisle.

The startled bride and groom both looked at each other and then behind them. They then directed their gaze towards the man who had raised an objection.

'It must be some nutcase. I don't know this person,' whispered Zoe to Spencer.

'No, I have never met him either,' whispered back Spencer.

Spencer by then had realised that these were law enforcers. He was also aware that his time was up and that he would not be walking back down the isle with his new bride, but instead would be accompanied with a couple of police officers.

'Who are you and why the intrusion?' asked the priest.

'I'm Detective Inspector Hallet of Her Majesty's police force,' replied Hallet.

'Why, do you wish to stop this marriage?' asked the priest.

'I have reason to believe that the groom is already married, is a serial bigamist and is about to commit bigamy again here in this church before this congregation,' replied Hallet.

The congregation were stunned. They had never seen a wedding stopped in mid ceremony before and murmurings started going around the church. All eyes were trained upon Spencer to witness his reaction and see what he was going to do next. Spencer just looked at the floor of the church waiting for the officers to come and arrest him.

'This wedding is suspended, you must continue with your investigations and carry out the duties you must do,' the priest said to Hallet.

When the two men arrived Spencer put both his hands forward in readiness for the handcuffs to be clamped upon his wrists. He offered no resistance as he walked down the isle with the two officers either side of him.

Zoe in the meantime was becoming hysterical shouting out to the two officers accompanying her groom.

'There must be some mistake, do you hear me? You have made a grave error. You will pay for this,' yelled Zoe.

The two officers ignored Zoe's protestations and pushed Spencer into a waiting car. Zoe rushed towards them trying to pull Spencer from them, but in her weakened state was easily overpowered.

'Well you've spoilt the wedding, but you are not going to ruin the honeymoon. When you realise that you have made a mistake, I will expect you to send him back to me in an hour's time with an apology,' yelled Zoe to the two detectives.

Both Spencer and the two detectives ignored Zoe's ranting as they got into the police car and drove away.

'How did you know where to find me?' said Spencer curious about how they discovered he was getting married.

'Karen told us you were getting married in the local church, so we followed her advice,' replied Hallet.

'That's very surprising. I have never spoken to Karen in a long time. How did she know I was getting married, and if she did know, how was she aware that it was today and in that church? Also how did she know the time the ceremony commenced?' quizzed Spencer

'Oh, we don't reason on the advice we are given, we just follow it,' replied Hallet.

As the car continued to the police station, Spencer was puzzled on how Karen could have been so informed on the details of the wedding especially as he hadn't informed anyone.

Chapter 25 Questions

Andrews was led into a tiny room by detective Hallet and later accompanied by detective Foster. The room lacked air and there wasn't a lot of light. The three men sat round a square table. It appeared that Hallet was going to ask all the questions whilst Foster was going to write down notes.

'Sit down Andrews. We have a few questions we would like to put to you, but first we must caution you, that what ever you say here today, may at some future date be used in evidence against you. Do you understand?' said Hallet.

'Yes,' said Andrews as he fidgeted on his seat.

'Now do you want a solicitor present whilst we go through the questions?' asked Hallet.

'No, that won't be necessary,' replied Spencer.

'Also at the end of this interview a statement will be compiled which we will ask you to sign. Do you understand?' asked Hallet.

Spencer acknowledged his agreement with a nod of the head.

'Now before we start. Is there anything you want to ask us? enquired Hallet.

'Yes there is. Onomatopoeia. What a ridiculous word that is,' said Spencer.

'Sorry, on-a-mat-a-pee-a, onomatopoeia? Hallet said the word in syllables slowly and then repeated it quickly. I don't know what you are talking about. Do you know what he is talking about Foster,' said Hallet.

'I haven't a clue, I'm sure it's nothing to do with what he is in here for,' replied Foster.

'Do you mean to say that neither of you have never heard of the word,' said Spencer.

'No it means nothing to me,' replied Hallet.

'Nor me,' admitted Foster.

'I thought everyone knew the word and what it meant,' said Spencer.

'Well, I'm not even going to ask what it means or anything about the word. Can we get on with it,' replied Hallet.

'You, Mr. Hallet have restored my faith in human nature.   I'm not a numb brain after all,' said Spencer.

'Well that remains to be seen.   I'll let you know after you have answered some of our questions. We get some very peculiar people in here sometimes,' said Hallet.

A smile of delight came over Spencer's face, he had actually proven that there was at least two other people in the world that didn't know what this word meant; the word which he had developed a particular fascination.

'Can we get on with what we are here to do?   Now, let me see,' continued Hallet as he looked through his documents.   'Your name is Spencer Henry Andrews, you are a lorry driver and you are married to Glenda Andrews. Is that correct?'

'Yes,' said Andrews.   'I married Glenda twenty one years ago.'

'So why would you want to marry Karen and proceed to marry Zoe? Are you a serial bigamist?' asked Hallet.

'Yes, I suppose you could call me that,' admitted Andrews, believing that as he was caught he had nothing to hide.

'In that case are there any others besides the three I have mentioned, where you have embarked on a wedding ceremony?' asked Hallet.

Andrews remained silent and just stared at the table top wondering whether he should admit the other offences.

'I must warn you that if there are others, you would be best served to tell us now, as we will be certain to find out the truth at a later date,' insisted Hallet.

'Okay,' said Andrews, 'there was also Holly, Iris, Janet, and Linda.'

Hallet looked at Foster in sheer disbelief, as if he hadn't heard right.

'Are you trying to be funny?' asked Hallet who was losing patience with Spencer.

'No! I really did marry these women and they are backed up by marriage certificates.

'Gosh,' said Hallet, 'that totals six wives in all. You have been busy, I wasn't expecting that.'

'Why in God's name would you want to marry all of these women Spencer Henry Andrews?' asked Hallet.

'Well if my namesake Henry, who was once part of the royal nobility can get away with it, then so can I,' replied Spencer.

'I don't know what you mean,' said Hallet.

'My second name is Henry. You will remember, Henry Tudor the King of England in the sixteenth century had six wives and he beheaded two of those he didn't want. All of mine with the exception of one are still living,' said Andrews who was happy to elucidate with the question.

'What surnames did you adopt for your new brides?'

'Could you rephrase that for me?' asked Andrews.

'Well let's put it this way. Serial bigamists don't normally use their own surnames when they remarry, as they can easily be detected,' said Hallet.

'Oh I see,' said Andrews. 'Well there was Butcher, Chandler, Drake, Evans and Fitzgerald.'

'Were there any children as a result of these partnerships,' asked Hallet.

'Oh yes,' admitted Andrews who recited a list of his thirteen children from his well preserved list which he drew from his pocket.

'I see you have to rely on notes to recall the names of your family,' commented Hallet.

'Yes, there are a lot of names to remember, so I have found it necessary to write them all down,' replied Spencer.

'Are you getting all this down,' asked Hallet as he directed the question to Foster who was scribbling as fast as Spencer could list the names.

'Oh yes, I think I see the pattern that is emerging here looking at this list. You won't believe this. This is incredible and almost unbelievable,' said Foster as he looked amazed at the information he had recently written down.

'I bet they call you **'the alphabet man,'** don't they,' continued Foster directing the question to Andrews.

'I don't know what you are alluding. Is that some kind of joke?' asked Andrews who was mystified by Foster's comment.

'No joke. Well listen to this,' said Foster. 'Your name is Andrews and you changed it five times to Butcher, Chandler, Drake, Evans and Fitzgerald for the purpose of marriage ceremonies. You married legally once to Glenda where you used your own surname 'Andrews' for the ceremony. Nothing wrong in that. You then went on to illegally marry Holly, Iris, Janet, Karen and Linda using the pseudonyms for surnames I have just mentioned. With these partners you begat thirteen children which are named in age order, Malcolm, Norma, Olga, Patricia, Quilly, Richard, Stanley, Thomas, Ursula, Vera, William, Xavia and Yvonne. The marriage that was about to occur yesterday, which we managed thankfully to stop, was with a woman called Zoe. If you take the first letter of each name, you discover a distinct sequence.'

'I'm sorry, I have completely lost you,' replied Andrews who was not aware of the point Foster was making, but desperately trying to make some sense of it.

'Just refer back to the notes you have in your hand. You my friend in using the first letter of every Surname and Christian name I mentioned, from the information you've given us, have completely gone through the alphabet from 'A' to 'Z' in a chronological sequence, with the names of partners and offspring without missing a single letter.'

'Curious,' said Andrews as he looked at the list on the note paper he had in his hand, 'I knew that the five false names I was using as surnames was in an alphabetical sequence because I picked them, but I was not aware that the partners I chose had any sequential connotation and must be purely coincidental. After all my partner's names were chosen by their parents. Neither was I aware that my children's names had any alphabetical seriatim, as all the names were chosen by my partners who knew nothing of each others existence.'

'If what you are saying is right, then the chances of this happening as a complete coincidence must run into something like at least a billion to one chance,' remarked Hallet.

'Well would you credit that,' said Spencer having difficulty in believing what had just been pointed out to him.

'Well, whatever it was, coincidence or not, it's gratifying to know that we have put a stop to your bigamist capers,' said Hallet.

'If we hadn't caught you, would you have continued marriage many more times over and adopted names using an alphabetical sequence again, because clearly you have used up all the letters the first time around,' continued Hallet.

'I don't have to answer that question,' said Andrews who was aware that Hallet had reduced the questioning to sarcasm.

'No, I don't suppose you do,' replied Hallet with a smirk.

There was a long silence which Hallet broke.

'You do realise don't you that we will have to inform all your partners, five of whom went through bogus marriage ceremonies. You said earlier that your partners never knew of each others existence. Well Spencer Andrews, they will know soon,' warned Hallet.

'Yes, I know. In a way I am relieved that it will all come out in the open, it will take a lot of pressure off me, as I have always found it difficult to satisfy all the demands made by my wives and when they know the truth they will be aware why I couldn't sustain a full family life with any of them. However I did my very best,' said Andrews.

'Well it's a good job you are in custody under the full protection of the law, otherwise I feel you could be exposed to a lynch mob,' remarked Hallet.

'Since I married my second wife Holly, I've been living on the edge,' confided Andrews.

'Living on the edge of what?' asked Hallet.

'It feels like I'm living on the edge of a cliff precipice, ready to topple over at any time,' said Spencer.

'You have two sons in the police force, in fact they work in this constabulary. What are they going to think about the crimes you have committed?' asked Hallet.

'It terrifies me that they and the rest of my children will learn the truth, but it must be remembered that I am still their father and had I not broken the law, then nine of my thirteen children would not be here today. They are all working, so you could say that

I have provided a valued service to the community,' replied Spencer.

'Yes, but what about the four that were borne to Glenda, your legal wife. Haven't they a right to be angry?' asked Hallet.

'Yes, I suppose they have, but I hope in due time they will forgive me,' replied Andrews.

'Now. What about Linda, the last person who entered a marriage ceremony with you?' enquired Hallet.

'Linda, my sixth wife died six years ago. I am glad that she will not be exposed to these revelations, so in reality you will only need to inform four wives that they went through bogus marriages,' said Andrews.

'What I cannot understand is why you should want to marry so many women?' enquired Hallet.

'In a way I didn't want to marry any of them, I had at one time resigned myself to being a confirmed bachelor. Looking back I see that circumstances forced me into serial marriages. In doing my best to please people, I began to think that marriage was the answer,' explained Andrews.

'I am not going to pretend that I understand what you have just said. However I can inform you of this. You could be put away for a long time over what you have done,' advised Hallet.

'It's all academic now, because even if you jail me for the offence, my life is shortly about to be extinguished from me, so I will never do the full term that any judge will want to impose on me. You see I have an advanced level of AIDS, so I am not expected to live that long,' confided Andrews who was shivering and coughing uncontrollably.'

'Why then would you want to get married if you have a disease that you can pass onto a partner,' asked Foster.

'Because she, Zoe, is also infected,' said Andrews, 'so it is nothing I can pass onto her. In fact she originally gave it to me. You could call it just deserves for the life I have lived and the heartache I have inflicted on others.'

'What about your real wife. That is the first person you married and the other women. Don't you think that they need some protection against you?' asked Foster.

'If you are referring to the disease that I have, I stopped sexual contact with them long ago as soon as I knew I was HIV infected. It wouldn't be right to knowingly infect any of them. Plus none of them deserve it,' said Andrews.

'It's true, you don't look at all well. I will get a doctor to check you out. In the meantime I will have to return you to your cell until your case comes up, which will be next Tuesday in four days time,' said Foster.

'While I am here, I would like to report another crime involving a Mr. James Walker,' said Spencer.

'Why do you want to bring his name into this?' asked Foster.

'Because he has been extorting money from me by blackmail, which is a crime,' replied Spencer.

'Can you prove this?' asked Foster.

'Yes. My bank statements show regular payments made out to his account,' replied Spencer.

'I assume the blackmail is all to do with keeping your bigamist activities a secret,' said Foster.

'Yes that's right, although he was only aware of the bogus marriage to his sister Karen, he knew nothing of the other weddings that took place,' replied Spencer.

'We will follow it up. He has got quite a shock coming to him,' confirmed Foster.

'Well?' asked Spencer.

'Well what?' asked Foster.

'You said you would confirm whether I was a numb brain or not, after I answered all your questions, which I have done,' said Spencer.

'No. I don't believe you are anything of the sort. I think you really did know what you were doing, but were fearful of the consequences if you got caught,' replied Foster.

After the short interrogation to which Spencer Andrews had given full co-operation, he was returned to his cell and the door banged firmly shut and locked. It was there that he was left alone to contemplate his life of bigamy and the lives he destroyed as a result of his selfishness and egoistic nature. His thoughts turned to each one of them and the good times he shared. He also thought about his thirteen children and hoped that they would not judge him too harshly for the crimes he had committed to their mothers.

In the cell, Spencer felt very cold and wrapped his arms around his skeletal frame. The blotches which appeared on his skin were getting worse and itching all over. He had a swelling in his neck, under his armpits and groin. His nose was running badly as if he had a heavy cold and his whole body ached. After ten minutes he climbed into his bunk fighting for breath, shivering, and unable to stop his whole body shaking.

The following day an officer went to check on Spencer Andrews and found him lying half on his bunk with his upper body slumped on the floor. His head was on one side and his eyes were open. On further investigation it was found that Spencer, the alphabet man, the name dubbed by the police force, had departed quietly from this world. His death must have occurred some time during the night. Spencer had evaded the wrath of all the partners he took into a wedding ceremony. He had also dodged the embarrassing questions in court which would have inevitably attained public notoriety. He had achieved one thing. He had escaped the British penal system which was something he desperately tried to avoid all his life.

Spencer's death had cheated them all, Jim, the wives, and the families of the wives from a satisfactory retribution.

*

Hallet, who agreed to follow up Spencer's report that James Walker was extracting money through the crime of blackmail, called at Karen's house to establish his whereabouts. When he did eventually catch up with the offender, Jim denied all knowledge of the crime of which he was being accused.

'Mr. Walker, we have been informed by Spencer Andrews that you have been blackmailing him over several years,' said Hallet.

'Why would I blackmail my brother-in-law, that's a terrible thing to accuse me of,' said Jim.

'According to Spencer Andrews, you were blackmailing him for a bigamist crime,' said Hallet.

'Well, it's news to me. I didn't know he was a bigamist,' replied Jim who was quavering in his voice.

'It seems that it is your word against his,' said Hallet.

'I didn't know he was a bigamist. Do you mean to say he cheated on my sister?' enquired Jim who tried to act surprised.

Hallet completely ignored the question, not wishing to waste his time on providing information to which he was sure Jim was aware.

'Well, it is easy for us to check. All we have to do is ask the bank to give us a copy of your bank statement and if it indicates regular weekly payments coming out of Spencer's account and going into your account, then we know that we will have to take Spencer's word for it,' confirmed Hallet.

Jim realising that the police force could easily find the information they were looking for, decided that there was no point in lying about it.

'Alright, I admit it, I did know he was a bigamist. I did ask Spencer for money, but only because of the bad way he treated my sister,' replied Jim, who felt that Hallet had sufficient information on him to be arrested.

Jim was then clamped in handcuffs and led away.

Karen learning of her brother's crime was furious that he could stoop so low as to extort money out of her partner. She quickly came to the conclusion that Jim's greed had prevented her from receiving a better living allowance from Spencer.

Chapter 26   The Wives

Hallet, had the unenviable task of informing the wives of the alphabet man's death and more importantly the crime he had committed against all of them.

Although Karen and Glenda knew of each others existence in their relationship to Spencer, they were nevertheless aghast that they were not the only ones who were sharing this man.   Holly and Janet was also aware that they were married to the same person, but Holly not knowing about Glenda believed her marriage to be legal.   Zoe believed that in her wedding being stopped she had had a lucky escape,   however her illness was terminal so she wasn't expected to live long anyway.

The others were equally shocked and partly in disbelief at the revelations they were hearing from Hallet.

Glenda, the only legal married wife, arranged the funeral and invited all the other women whom Spencer had formed a bogus wedding ceremony, which included Zoe, who's marriage had come to an abrupt end by the long arm of the law.   Glenda had previously survived one shock and out of all the other women she was the strongest to overcome the latest revelation. She had received so many bombshells in the past from Spencer regarding the presence of another wife, Karen and the possibility that she might be HIV infected, that she had become used to receiving bad news regarding her relationship with her husband and treated it as just another problem to overcome.

The church was filled with all Spencer's five surviving partners and his thirteen children. Also attending the ceremony was Spencer's mother and father who hadn't shared the secret life of their son. Although they were dumbfounded by the news of Spencer's marital exploits, they were nevertheless pleased that they had so many grandchildren, which was something they felt was missing in their lives.

There was, however, one additional member of the family that Spencer never met and that was a girl born to Patricia and William. The couple agreed that they could not terminate a life, no matter how illegal the circumstances that dominated their decision. As Zoe never managed to become a member of Spencer's expanding family, this left a gap for a name at the end of the alphabet, so in true tradition Patricia and Williams named their little girl Zelda, thereby completing the sequence.

Glenda who was given the prestigious list by Hallet that Spencer compiled and kept in his cab headed 'My Family', added Zelda's name to the bottom with the words 'granddaughter' in brackets. This latest entry completed Spencer's list.

Indeed, Spencer truly could be termed as the Alphabet Man, the name dubbed by Foster having discovered the extraordinary progression of letters in the family names.

There were two notable absentee's at the church service, Jim Walker who was arrested following information provided by Spencer and Holly's father Harold Winters who saw Spencer's death as a valuable contribution to the community as well as a welcome relief to Holly.

At the funeral big arguments erupted amongst the wives, who couldn't decide who was going to inherit his money as Spencer never left a will. The rowing went to fever pitch, with much finger pointing and raised voices. The disagreeing five needn't have concerned themselves about Spencer's wealth, because he died penniless and therefore had nothing to leave any of them.

It dawned on Iris, seeing so many of Spencer's family that she must have been contributing the living expenses to most of the mourners in the church and realised that it could have been the reason why she had gone from riches to poverty over a relatively short space of time. This made her very angry even though there was no one there that she could vent her anger on.

Holly always believed that she was the only legitimate bride of Spencer and was devastated to learn that she was not and that Glenda was married before her.

Karen, who exposed the secret of Spencer's bigamy to the police was shocked to learn that he hadn't just committed the crime once but another five times. Janet was equally dumbfounded in being made aware that she had been sharing Spencer with five other women when initially she believed that there was only one other woman and that was Holly.

The five women continued to argue at the graveside.

Then amongst all the arguing, Glenda stepped forward holding one arm up in the air.

'Stop! I expect Spencer is looking down on us now having a good belly laugh at us all arguing and the mess he has left behind for us all to sort out.'

Karen, looked up at the sky and said, 'Spencer you have made fools of all of us, it is now time to stop and let us get on with our lives in peace and without interference.'

Following Karen's example Janet looked up to the sky and said, 'but that's not going to happen is it Spencer? You will plague our lives in both thought and deed until we all turn to dust.'

Suddenly without warning, there was a clap of thunder and a lightening flash which struck the metal conductor on the church roof. A cloud burst then quickly followed which drenched all those in the cortege heading away from the grave.

Was this a sign of the alphabet man answering Janet's claims of ridiculing the prospect of calm or was it a coincidental natural force?

We will never know.

------------------------The End------------------------